NEIGH

NEIGHBOURS

Carl Ruhen

From an original concept by Reg Watson and based on the scripts of Alan Coleman, Coral Drouyn, Penny Fraser, Valda Marshall, Christine McCourt, David Phillips, Betty Quin, Patrea Smallacombe, Hugh Stuckey, Adrian van den Bok, Reg Watson, Sally Webb, Craig Wilkins

A STAR BOOK
published by
the Paperback Division of
W.H. ALLEN & Co. Plc

A Star Book
Published in 1987
by the Paperback Division of
W.H. Allen & Co. Plc
44 Hill Street,
London W1X 8LB

Printed and bound in Great Britain by
Anchor Brendon Ltd, Tiptree, Essex

ISBN 0 352 32110 5

1

A suburb . . .

There isn't much to distinguish this suburb from the one next to it, or the ones to the north and south of it. There is no sudden or dramatic encounter with it; it is just there, spreading out over a few square miles, streets intersecting, houses clustered together – and from any vantage point, if one were to be found, the glitter of back yard swimming pools in the sunlight. It is not a rich suburb, nor is it a poor one; it is not particularly old, nor one of the mushrooming estates where, not very far away and until recently, there had been fields and paddocks with bushland beyond.

It is a suburb unevenly dissected by the railway; there is a main street and a shopping mall with parking space for more than a thousand cars, a post office and branch offices for more than half a dozen banks and building societies. The council chambers were built on the site of the

5

original building more than 70 years ago, and a new building will soon be constructed to cope more effectively with the demands of a steadily growing population.

In this suburb there are market gardens and a new retirement centre; there is a pub (mock Tudor, built in 1937), a bowling club and an RSL Club; there is a community centre, an Olympic-sized swimming pool and a municipal library. There are parks with neatly laid out flower beds, and schools and churches. Most of the streets are tree lined.

During the summer months, the weather can be very hot and dry. In the winter heavy morning frosts are not uncommon in this suburb distant from the coast where, with the prevailing sea breezes, the temperatures are less extreme.

At one time the area comprised mainly market gardens and orchards, a few of which still remain on the outskirts and in the path of the new sub-divisions. Some of the houses built by the original settlers are still standing, but these are mostly run down and decrepit, earmarked for eventual demolition to make way for new development.

One of the original settlers in the area was old Jack Ramsay, who had an orchard and was a member of the original council when the municipality received its charter just before the turn of the century – a position he held, twice serving as mayor, for almost 50 years. For his service to the community, Jack Ramsay is commemorated by the street which bears his name and in which his grandson still lives with his family, roughly on the site of the old man's original homestead. Max Ramsay has always been fiercely proud of the association; his attitude towards the street and its residents is proprietorial to no small degree. There are some elements among the residents he would prefer not to see, but it is a sad fact of life that he can do little more than show his disapproval in small but nevertheless marked ways. Okay, so there are husbands who beat their wives, there's an alcoholic or two, or people who have noisy parties – and while these were the sorts of hazards that could be found just about everywhere, he just wished they didn't have to be found in *his* street. Therefore, when a stripper moved into the house next door but one, he wasn't at all pleased. In fact, he was quite angry about it; a female who took off her clothes for money was not the sort of person who was needed in Ramsay Street which was, by and large, a respectable thoroughfare.

By rights, if everything had gone according to plan, Des Clarke would have been living there at Number 28 with his new bride, settling in quite nicely among the brand new furniture and appliances with which the place had been stocked preparatory to what everyone had thought would be a life of pleasant conformity and kids and the

7

prospect of periodic promotion at the bank where Des was already the chief accountant. There was no reason to suppose that he wouldn't be seen on Sunday mornings mowing his lawn or washing the car, cleaning the pool, pruning the trees or laying out a rockery, and in time playing with the kids. There was certainly no reason to suppose that at the very last minute, on the morning of the wedding itself, and after the rowdy stag party that had gone on until the early hours of the morning and had kept much of the street awake, the bride should suddenly have second thoughts and call the whole thing off.

For Max Ramsay, the noise of the party had been bad enough – he had been up many times, ringing Jim Robinson next door and demanding to know what he intended to do about these bloody neighbours of his who were making all that racket. Jim said reasonably, come on, mate, it's the poor guy's last night of freedom, give them a break. In the end Max had gone there himself, after two in the morning, and this girl he had never seen before had stormed out of the front door of Number 28, saying angrily to Des, the groom-to-be, who had followed her to the door, that if *that* was what he called kidding then they had picked the wrong girl for sure, and then when Max had started to remonstrate about the noise, had told him to drop dead, before heading off to her car in high dudgeon. All that had been bad enough, but when he learnt later that the stripper (who had been hired for the party – *and* by his own son, for God's sake – and who had told him to drop dead), was actually moving in with Des, he had been appalled. What made it worse was that it was his own idea.

Not that he had been thinking of the stripper – her name was Daphne – when he suggested to Des that since Lorraine had decided not to go through with the wedding, leaving Des not only with a king-sized hangover, but also puzzled and worried and with a hefty mortgage, he might think about taking in a couple of lodgers to offset the expenses.

Des and Jim Robinson had worked out that with Lorraine's contribution, Des would be up for an extra couple of hundred bucks a week – and for Max the solution had been simple. There was no need for Des to worry and look so miserable about it. 'Get a couple of people to share,' he had suggested. 'Two blokes, fifty bucks a week, and you're laughing.' And Jim Robinson had thought that wasn't such a bad idea and Max, carried away by the simplicity of it, had said it was a ripper. Two blokes, he had said, and two blokes was what he had really meant – not a stripper called Daphne who had told him to drop dead the night before the wedding that wasn't a wedding.

And she had been in Des's house even then, that morning after the wedding had been called off. She had come back to look for her watch which she had mislaid somewhere, then stayed on to help Des clean up the mess. When she had come into the room where Max and Jim Robinson were sorting out Des's financial problems, and told Des she was off now, and Des had said, thanks for everything, Daphne, Max had looked at her, and the penny had dropped because Jim Robinson had told him there had been a stripper at the bucks' party, because that was the normal thing apparently. He had put two and two together because this was the same girl who had told him to drop dead, and said, in a tone of revelation, 'Hey, you're the stripper, aren't you?'

'No,' she had replied. 'I'm Daphne Lawrence.'

And Jim Robinson had said, 'Thanks for your help, Daphne.'

Max had looked from one to the other. There was something going on here he didn't know about. 'What help?'

'She's been helping me,' Des had explained.

Aha. 'Didn't take you long, did it?' he had challenged Des who should have been on his honeymoon by now – and, of course, that was more money down the drain, if he couldn't get a refund from the travel agent. They had planned to go to the Barrier Reef for their honeymoon.

'Now look, Mr Ramsay ...'

'Ramsay?' Daphne had looked suddenly alert,

and that was the moment when Shane had decided to make an appearance. 'He couldn't be your father, could he?' Daphne had asked Shane, jerking her head in Max's direction, and Max had demanded to know what Shane had to do with a woman like that.

'Well, everything, I guess,' Shane had answered. 'I booked her.'

Which was bloody lovely, his own son being mixed up with a stripper, and not only that, but a stripper who told him to drop dead when all he wanted was a bit of peace and quiet at two o'clock in the morning. 'Flaming strippers,' he had muttered when she had gone, and Shane had gone after her. Des had told him to relax because there wouldn't be any more stag parties.

'Yeah, well, there had better not be,' Max had growled. 'You start letting girls like that in a street like ours and it gets a bad name.'

The first inkling he had had that she had thoughts about moving into the street came when she had come down to the pool that morning to watch Shane training, doing his somersaults and pikes off the high board while Max watched him critically, putting him through his paces, working him hard, as he worked him hard every morning because he had high hopes for him, nothing short of the Olympics no less. Anyway, the girl, Daphne, the stripper, was there that morning as Shane performed his flawless manoeuvres off the

11

diving board, spinning and twisting and hardly making a splash as he entered the water – and Max didn't like her being there. He didn't like the way the two of them were being so friendly and, of course, it went back to the night of the stag party in Des's house, when Shane must have invited her to come down to the pool to watch him in training.

'Well, what do you think?' Shane had gasped, pulling himself out of the pool, water streaming off his body and making puddles on the ground.

'Very impressive,' Daphne had said. 'Now I'd better be on my way.'

'What's the hurry?'

'I want to see Des,' she had told him. 'I don't want to miss out on that room.'

'What room?' Max had asked suspiciously.

It was Shane who replied. 'Daphne's hoping to rent the room at Des's place.'

Max had stared at her. He had stared at Shane. What was this? The room at Des's place? This girl? This ... this ... *stripper*? No, that wasn't on. 'Now look,' he had yelped. 'Des is only renting to *blokes*. And they'd need top notch references.'

'Don't worry, Mr Ramsay,' Daphne had said with a sweet smile. 'I'll talk him round.'

Talk Des around, but not Max. That was what he had told her.

'Oh, I see.' She had raised her eyebrows. Cool as a cucumber she had been. '*You* own the house, do you?'

Of course he didn't, and if she really wanted to know what it had to do with him, well, he would tell her. There was no way he was having a stripper living in his street.

'Oh, so it's the *street* you own?'

'No, not that, either, but he would have her know that it *was* named after his grandfather, and that had to mean something, it gave him a say in what went on in the street.

And later that morning, back at Number 24, when Maria told him it wasn't really any of their business if the girl moved into Des's house, he had retorted that it certainly *was* their business if their son became involved with her – and what would Maria have to say about *that* if it happened? And Maria, preparing a large pot of soup, had said that if Shane became involved with *any* girl, it was his choice and his choice alone. 'Well, *I'll* have something to say, just you wait,' Max had said with some heat.

If that was his wife's attitude, Jim Robinson's reaction hadn't been much better when Max, thinking the news would come as a big surprise, had asked him if he knew that the stripper was trying to move in with Des Clarke. Oh yes, Jim had replied, he had already been talking to her about it, and what was more, she had struck him as being a nice type of girl.

When Max had tried to point out that the

reputation of the street would suffer, and that it could even be that property values would take a nosedive, never mind what some of the neighbours would think about her, Jim Robinson had suggested that they didn't need to worry too much about the wowsers, and as far as the neighbours were concerned, he thought that most of them would welcome the girl.

Max hadn't believed what he had just heard. In all the years he had known him, he had never thought Jim Robinson would welcome a girl like that into the street. But then, as Maria had reminded him, Jim was a very compassionate man, which Max didn't think was very helpful at all.

Now, despite all his objections, Daphne had moved in with Des Clarke – as a paying lodger, it was emphasised, but Max had his own thoughts about that – and, to his disgust, Max realised he had to live with the fact that there was a stripper living at Number 28 Ramsay Street. He was sure his old grandfather was turning over in his grave.

2

Scott Robinson tried not to show the deep disappointment he felt. He thought he had made it clear to Kim that he was inviting her out to dinner and a movie afterwards, but she had just told him she couldn't stay out that long, that she had to get back home in an hour or two because she had told her mother she was just going out for a walk. 'I'm sorry, Scott,' she said unhappily. 'I guess I didn't realise . . .'

Well, if she couldn't stay out tonight, Scott thought, putting the best face he could on this set-back, then at least they had the afternoon to themselves. 'No worries,' he said with a cheerfulness he didn't altogether feel. 'No, no worries.' Just a couple of hours at most. 'How about an ice cream?' he suggested.

'Sure.'

He had been looking forward to it all week and this afternoon, spruced up and ready to go out on his big date, his grandmother had told him he was looking cool, which was a bit of a surprise coming from her, and his father had handed him twenty bucks as an advance, he said, for the work Scott had been doing in the garden. He had told them last night he was taking a chick out for dinner, and when his dad had raised his eyebrows and looked at Scott's grandmother, she had told him it was the first time Scott had taken a chick out for dinner, and there always had to be a first time. Even if he was only 15 years old, she didn't think he was too young to start taking chicks out to dinner. At times his grandmother could be quite modern in her thinking.

'Do I know her?' his Dad had asked.

'It's Kim Taylor,' Scott had replied. 'Her mother's a teacher at school.' That's how it was – he was in love with a girl who sat two rows in front of him in the classroom, and her mother was the teacher, which didn't leave him much scope, particularly with Mrs Taylor being the sort of teacher she was, being the sort of *woman* she was.

'A teacher, eh?' His father had been impressed. 'Well, if you want to bring this girl home any time, you know she'd be welcome.'

Scott had become nervous then. 'You won't ring her, or anything? The mother, I mean.'

'Why not?'

'Kim hasn't told her we're going out yet.'

'So what are you going to do about that?' his father had asked, giving him a shrewd look.

'That's up to Kim.'

'No,' his father had said. 'It's up to both of you.'

Yeah, well... From what he knew of Kim's mother, that was a real challenge. Kim had told him about her mother, and how she was always keeping an eye on her, always wanting to know where she was, what she was doing, warning her about this and that, warning her about boys, what to do and what not to do, generally just being heavy on her all the time.

The ice cream parlour was new, with white tiles and potted plants and girls behind the counter wearing red and white uniforms. Scott bought two ice creams – chocolate for him, pistachio for her – and then, sitting in the corner, shielded from the street by the plants, they ate their ice cream and discussed what they would do next. Scott asked her, and Kim shyly said she didn't mind, what would *he* like to do? And Scott said, but I asked you first – and then someone else replied, what would you like to do, which brought the falsetto response, what would *you* like to do, and the first voice continued, just behind the pot plants, 'But I asked you first.'

Then, to Scott's dismay, the faces that belonged to the voices were peering through the pot plants at them – and Scott thought, bloody hell, it was just like *them* to show up, Danny Ramsay and his mate Eddie Sherwin. That afternoon, Danny had been put out when Scott had told him that he couldn't go with him to Eddie's to play around with the tape recorder, editing the tapes to change the context and the meaning of the recorded conversation, which had been a bit of a fad with them lately. He noticed they had the tape recorder with them. They must have been following him and Kim, squatting there behind the pot plants, listening to their conversation such as it was, being concerned only with where the other wanted to go, and neither of them coming up with any suggestions.

'Come on,' Scott said, standing up. 'Let's get out of here.'

They got out of there, and headed for the reserve where Scott knew a place where they could be private.

They walked through the reserve, down a narrow track and across a dry creek bed, which they followed for some distance in the direction of the new sub-divisions. They came to another track leading away from the creek bed, and began to climb.

Kim told Scott that her mother had hit the roof when she had informed her the day before that she was going to the pictures. Her mother had decided she wasn't going to the pictures, and that was that. When she had appealed to her father, her mother had chipped in and said that Kim's father agreed with her, and that was that, too.

Kim had been angry. Her father was so completely under her mother's thumb, she said and Scott agreed that that was too bad.

At the top of the rise the land levelled out. A short distance in front of them were the crumbling remains of an old stone building. 'What is this place?' Kim asked as they approached it.

'It's an old monastery,' Scott told her.

'Are you sure it's all right?' Kim asked doubtfully.

'Sure thing. Nobody comes near the place now.'

The building was falling to pieces. There was no roof and blocks of stone lay in the long grass where they had fallen. Scott sensed Kim's nervousness. While she was looking away he disappeared into the building.

'Scott,' he heard her calling when she discovered he was missing. 'Scott.' Her voice was rising in panic. 'Come on, where are you?'

In the shadows, just behind the doorway, Scott gave a long, low moan. Kim turned and saw him. Scott laughed. 'Come on, admit it. You were scared, weren't you?'

'I was *not* scared.'

'Not even just a little?' He was standing just inside the doorway. She couldn't see his hand as it moved up to the back of his head.

'Not even just a little.'

'Yes, you ... aaaah.'

All she could see from where she was standing was the hand grabbing his hair and dragging him back into the shadows. He screamed and began to struggle. 'Help me!' he cried.

'Scott!' He lay face down in the shadows, grinning broadly; it was a good act, and if that didn't frighten her ... 'Scott, are you all right?' Yes, now he could tell from her voice that she was scared.

She came tentatively to the doorway. Scott lay still. 'Oh no,' he heard her groan, then, 'Scott? Can you hear me?' He didn't move. 'I'll get help.'

Then, before she could move away, he had rolled over and, grabbing her as she bent over him, twisted up onto his feet and kissed her. Startled, she jumped away from him. 'Oh ... *you*!'

Scott was laughing. 'Who said she wasn't scared? You really thought they had me, didn't you?'

Her fright had now given way to anger. 'You're very funny,' she said shortly. 'I'm going home.'

She turned and began to walk away. 'See you at school,' Scott called cheerfully after her.

'Drop dead,' she snapped without looking back. Smiling to himself, Scott waited. She would be back. He knew she would be back; there was something she had forgotten. He wondered how long it would take her to remember.

She hadn't even reached the trees before she remembered. She turned and came back. 'Oh, come back to apologise, have you?' Scott said.

Kim shook her head. 'You've got all my money – remember?'

That was right; she had handed it to him in the ice cream parlour. 'So I have,' he said as if he had forgotten all about it. 'How much was it again?'

'Ten dollars.'

He took the ten dollar note from his pocket and held it out to her. As she was taking it, he grasped her hand and held onto it. 'Sorry,' he said.

Kim smiled at him. 'Me, too.'

'Can we kiss and make up?'

'Okay.'

Scott kissed her. Her lips were cool and moist. Scott drew away and pointed to the side of the building. 'We could sit over there if you'd like.'

Kim was frowning a little. 'We'd better not.'

'Come on,' he urged, pulling her towards the wall. 'Just for a little while.'

She held back. 'No.'

'Okay.' Disappointed, Scott released her hand and moved away. 'Okay, forget it,' he said bitterly.

Now Kim was upset by his reaction. 'Scott, don't be like that.'

'Like what?'

'That's what you brought me here for, isn't it?' she said stiffly. 'Sex.'

'Yeah.' Scott laughed scornfully. 'I'm the school rapist.'

Kim stood there for a long moment as if undecided. 'I went to see the doctor,' she said quietly. 'To go on the pill.'

'The Pill?' Scott was puzzled. 'Why?'

'Because this sort of thing never happened to me before, that's why.'

'And what did he say?' Scott asked. 'Did he put you on the pill?'

'No, he talked me out of it.' There were tears in her eyes. 'I'm sorry . . .'

'Hey, hey.' Scott tried to cheer her up. 'It doesn't matter.' It really didn't matter. He put his arms around her and tried to comfort her as the tears began to flow.

If Scott felt bad about what had happened, he would have felt a whole lot worse if he had known that this conversation had been recorded by two kids who were absorbed by the current rage for editing tapes. But he had no idea that he and Kim had been followed from the ice cream parlour by Danny Ramsay and Eddie Sherwin to this crumbling old building that had once been a monastery, where Scott had told Kim no one came any more.

It had started off as a bit of a giggle, really; a little harmless fun. Danny had given Scott a demonstration of what could be done with a tape of Danny's Mum talking to his old man, and another of Max yelling at him, which Max did all the time. The result, after Eddie had done his tinkering with the tape, was that it seemed that Max was yelling at Maria who, in her turn, was just making pleasant conversation. 'Just wait until you hear what Eddie's working on *now*,' Danny said meaningfully.

When Scott did get to hear what Eddie had been working on, he was horrified. Kim, too, was horrified – and what was a thousand times worse was that Kim's mother was there to hear it as well, as indeed was the whole class. And it was Kim's mother who was responsible for it being made so public, to the shame and embarrassment of Kim and Scott, to the amusement of the rest of the class, and to the outrage of Mrs Taylor herself.

When she became aware that Danny Ramsay was smiling to himself when he shouldn't have been because the essay she had set for the class was on a serious topic, Mrs Taylor wondered why. She saw that he had his hand cupped over one ear, and as she moved up behind him, noticed that he was not writing. He looked up at her, startled and suddenly guilty, as she removed his hand from over his ear and then, seeing the wire leading from his ear, followed it to the desk immediately in front where Eddie Sherwin was sitting. She picked up the small tape recorder from Eddie's lap.

'Well, well, well, Eddie,' she said ominously.

'What have we here?'

Eddie was confused. He flushed. 'Sorry, Mrs Taylor.'

The rest of the class was watching with interest, their essays forgotten for the time being. Mrs Taylor was holding the recorder in the palm of her hand. 'Whatever's on the tape is obviously very funny,' she remarked. 'May we share the joke, Eddie?'

'No.' Eddie almost yelped the word.

'No?' Mrs Taylor's smile was deceptively languid.

'It's just some crazy stuff, Mrs Taylor.' Eddie was looking very guilty. Watching him, Scott wondered idly what could be on the tape to make him look so guilty. Surely not the edited exchange between Danny's Mum and Dad ... 'Just some some stuff we edited together over the weekend,' Eddie muttered almost inaudibly.

'Really?' There was something quite predatory about Mrs Taylor's smile. 'Then I think we should hear it. Perhaps it will give us an insight into that sense of humour of yours.'

Eddie was literally squirming on his chair. Danny wasn't looking too comfortable, either, Scott noted. 'I don't *want* to play the tape.'

Mrs Taylor's smile vanished. 'You'll do as you're told,' she snapped.

Eddie had no choice. Mrs Taylor was standing over him. Everybody waited to hear what was on the tape. Eddie looked around the room as if seeking help in his predicament. But there was no help. Mrs Taylor was waiting. Eddie pressed the 'Play' button, and a moment later Scott was shocked to hear his voice, and Kim's voice, filling the classroom.

It was the conversation he had had with Kim out at the old monastery – but it wasn't quite; it had been changed. He glanced quickly across at Kim. Her face had gone white; her eyes were wide and fearful. The words – Scott's and Kim's – were thrown into the room by the running tape.

'Scott, don't be like that.'

'I'm the school rapist.'

'That's what you brought me here for, isn't it? Sex.'

'Sure. How much was it again?'

'Ten dollars. I went to see a doctor. To go on the pill.'

And that was when Mrs Taylor, her face contorted with rage, screamed at Eddie to switch the thing off. Choking back her sobs, Kim stared wildly at Scott then ran out of the room. Scott ran after her.

He caught up with her at the gate. 'Hey, wait,' he cried, grabbing her arm. 'Hey, Kim, hold it there a moment.'

She was crying. 'How could they *do* a thing like that?' she gasped.

'I know, I know.' Scott was furious at what had

happened. 'I'll kill them,' he muttered savagely.

'My mother,' Kim sobbed desperately. 'What's she going to do?'

'We didn't do anything wrong, Kim.'

'Do you think she'll believe that?' She shook her head desperately from side to side. 'They made it all so... *dirty*.' She turned and began to run along the footpath, and this time Scott didn't try to stop her.

3

Danny blamed himself for the accident. If it hadn't been his idea, if he hadn't been so insistent that they go to the beach that afternoon then they wouldn't have been at that particular place at that particular time, and maybe his older brother would have gone on to become the Olympic gold medallist their father, probably even more so than Shane himself, wanted him to be. Danny blamed himself for the accident. What made it worse was that, at first, Shane hadn't even wanted to go to the beach with him.

But they had gone to the beach – and how was anyone to know that just as they were on their way back from the beach, the bank where Julie Robinson from next door worked and where Des Clarke was chief accountant, would be held up and robbed. How was anyone to know that this would result in a police chase through the streets of the suburb, a siren wailing, the cars – the getaway car, the pursuing police car, and Shane's car – all converging on a particular inter-section . . . ? Danny asked himself this over and over again – and still blamed himself.

He blamed himself, and his father blamed him. As if he hadn't already been in enough trouble, that girl Kim running away from home just because he and Eddie had fooled around with the tape they had made out at the old monastery that day, and there had been that fight with Scott, and the old man had come charging in like a wounded bull, pulled them apart, and started abusing *him* and not Scott who had started the fight. But that was pretty typical of Max – always blaming him for something, coming down heavy on him for this or that. Sometimes Danny thought his father reallly hated him.

Even when Danny had gone down to the pool that lunch time, to watch Shane training from the high board, his father had glowered at him. 'What the hell are *you* doing here?' he had demanded, and Danny had told him it was lunch time, that he thought he would come along and watch Shane for a while, and he had seen that Max was doing his best not to lose his temper.

He had watched Shane diving for a while, and Max had ignored him. Then Max had gone, and Shane had decided he had had enough training for one day. Danny had asked Shane to give him a lift to the beach. Shane had refused.

'Fantastic,' Danny had said sarcastically. 'My

own brother. So that's all the thanks I get for coming to watch you train.'

'You invited yourself.' Shane had been vigorously towelling himself dry.

'Will you do it?'

'Do what?'

'Run me to the beach.'

'Listen, I've already said I wouldn't, and I won't.' Shane had become impatient with him. 'Got better things to do with my time than run you to the beach, mate.'

But Danny had persisted, he had worn his older brother down, had told him that he needed a break from training, Mum was always saying he needed a break, all he ever did was training and gardening and why did he put up with all this gardening and training? Just to please Mad Max, that was why. And in the end he had gone to the beach with the budding Olympic champion who had enjoyed himself in the surf as much as Danny had.

And on their way home... The siren, the agonised screech of tyres, and Danny yelling as they came to the intersection and saw the cars speeding towards them from the opposite direction, 'Shane, look out!'

And then, some time later – he didn't know how much later, but it seemed that the echo of the sound of smashing glass and tortured metal was still reverberating around him and through him –

he had heard distant voices, had heard a siren becoming more distinct, (it might have been the same siren they had heard before the crash), and he had opened his eyes. He had been lying on the ground and someone in uniform was bending over him, and as the memory of what had happened came rushing back and he had struggled to sit up, ignoring the vicious stab of pain in his side, the man in the uniform – he had to be a policeman – had gently eased him back. 'It's all right, son. Don't move. The ambulance is coming now. Just don't move. You were lucky. You were thrown clear. You'll be all right.'

He had turned his head and seen the wreckage of the cars. 'Shane?' He had struggled to sit up again. 'Where is he? Where's my brother?' His first thought was that Shane had been killed in the collision.

Then, in the hospital, they had told him that Shane had been badly hurt, that he was being operated upon at that moment, and they would let Danny know as soon as there was anything to report.

'He's not going to die, is he?' Danny asked fearfully.

'Not if we can help it,' the doctor replied.

'It should be me,' Danny said miserably. 'I'm to blame.'

'You know that's not true,' the doctor gently admonished him. 'I'm sure the police explained

ree with every five litres.

Corgi edition of Jaguar's sensational 6 litre XJR-9. Castrol sponsored XJR-9's won both this year's
...es. But you'd better be quick; they've already captured pole position in your local accessory shop.

 Castrol

Offer only available on 5 litre Castrol GTX tins while stocks last.

Your cue... for a big snooker prize

How to enter

To play 'Starry Eyes', identify our four snooker aces from their eyes, pictured right.

A list of six famous names is provided for you to choose from. For example if you think eyes 1 belong to **A Dennis Taylor** then put A below 1 on the coupon and so on until you have identified all four sets of eyes. Add your name and address and send it to *TVTimes* Snooker 'Starry Eyes' Competition, PO Box 502, Leicester LE99 0AD,

to arrive no later than Friday, 16 September 1988. The first correct entry examined after the closing date will win the first prize. The next four correct will win £500 to invest.

Match the eyes to these snooker aces.

| A Dennis Taylor |
| B Jimmy White |
| C Stephen Hendry |
| D Willie Thorne |
| E Steve Davis |
| F Alex 'Hurricane' Higgins |

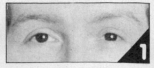

Rules

This competition is open to anyone resident in the UK aged 18 or over except employees and their families of Independent Television Publications Ltd, *TVTimes* printers, ITV programme companies and any other company connected with the competition. Entry must be in ink on an official entry coupon. No entry can be returned. No cash alternative for prizes. Holiday prize must be taken by 31 December 1989. Winners will be notified by post and results published in *TVTimes*. The decision of the editor is final. A list of winners is available on receipt of a stamped addressed envelope sent to *TVTimes* Snooker 'Starry Eyes' competition, PO Box 506, Leicester LE99 0AH.

To **TVTimes** Snooker 'Starry Eyes' Competition
PO Box 502, Leicester LE99 0AD

1	2	3	4
E	F		

Name..

Address..

....

................................Postcode....................

For further information on Fidelity Unit Trusts please tick ☐

BLOCK LETTERS, PLEASE   Closing date 16 September 1988

24

exactly what happened.'

Which wasn't the point at all. 'I *made* him drive me to the beach. If I hadn't kept at him we wouldn't have been there – and then that loony could have driven his car wherever he wanted.'

Danny's injuries weren't serious – a couple of broken ribs and a graze on his forehead where he had hit the road after being thrown clear of the car by the collision. He had been lucky.

'Now, look,' the doctor said, moving to the door. 'It's important that you rest, and it's not going to help you, or us, if you keep upsetting yourself over something that wasn't your fault.'

'Try telling that to my father,' Danny groaned.

The doctor opened the door. 'Your father's just arrived,' he told Danny. 'I'll bring him in as soon as I've spoken to him.'

But Max was the last person Danny wanted to see. 'No!' he cried. 'Please don't. I don't want to see him.' He wasn't even sure, however, if Max wanted to see *him*. Shane would be the one who he would be worrying about most – and Shane, no matter how much they tried to reassure Danny, was on the critical list. They were in there now, fighting to save his life.

The waiting was the worst part, the not knowing, and all he could do was lie in his bed, tightly bandaged, and in an agony of suspense. When the nurse came in to check his chart, she told him that Shane was still in the operating theatre. 'Doctor Lockyer told me you don't want to see your parents,' she said, replacing the chart at the end of the bed. 'Can you imagine how worried they are about you?' Danny said nothing; he didn't want to think about his parents – not his father, anyway. 'They're just down the corridor,' the nurse informed him. 'Can I bring them in?'

'No.'

'What about your mother? Will you see her?'

Danny thought about it, then nodded. Yes, all right then, he would see his mother.

Then his mother was there, sitting beside his bed, telling him to get well, that was all she wanted from him – and from Shane, too.

Danny turned his head on the pillow and looked directly into her eyes which were large and moist. 'You'd tell me if he was going to die, wouldn't you, Mum?'

'He's not going to die.' Her hands were clasped together. She spoke very softly.

'Maria.'

They turned their heads to the door where Max was standing. It was the first time Danny had seen his father since he had been brought to the hospital. He looked very subdued and worried. 'Shane wants to see you.'

Maria stood up and, bending over Danny, kissed him lightly on the cheek. 'I'll be back soon.'

Propped up against the pillows, Danny watched

as his mother stopped to say something to Max who shook his head. He heard his mother say, 'Please, Max,' and knew that she was urging him to speak to his son. But Max didn't want to speak to him – that much was obvious. Danny wished he would go away; there was nothing they had to say to each other.

Then his mother had gone and Max was advancing slowly into the room. Danny turned his head away and gazed through the window at the wall on the building opposite. 'Are you all right?' Max asked, and Danny could tell he was uncomfortable, that he didn't want to be there.

'Yeah.'

'Well... I'll be getting back to Shane then.' Max sounded relieved.

'Dad.' Danny turned his head again. Max was almost out of the room. He stopped and looked back at his son. 'Shane? What's happening? Please tell me the truth, Dad.'

'Tomorrow,' Max muttered evasively.

'Now, Dad. I want to know.'

'All right.' Max shrugged. 'If you really want to know...' Danny stared at him, waiting, fearing the worst. Max went on. 'He had a ruptured spleen and the doctors say he's got some spinal damage. They say he might be able to walk again, but...' he spread his hands in a gesture of resignation... 'no more diving.'

Danny slumped back against the pillows. It

was what he had feared. 'It should have been me, shouldn't it?' He couldn't have felt more miserable. 'Well, it wouldn't have mattered much, would it?' he persisted in the face of Max's silence, which was heavy and, to Danny, full of reproach. 'It should have been me. That's what we're both thinking, isn't it, Dad?'

Max said nothing. He stared at Danny for a long moment, then abruptly turned and left the room.

Later that afternoon, when the nurse brought a message from Shane asking Danny to come and see him, Danny refused. 'Tell him I can't make it yet.'

'I can take you through in a wheelchair,' the nurse suggested. 'Doctor Lockyer said it would be okay.'

'No. I don't want to.' Why didn't they leave him alone? Why did they have to keep pretending that things weren't really as bad as they were?

'What's the matter, Danny?'

'Nothing's the matter,' he muttered. 'I'm just not up to it yet, that's all.'

The nurse sighed. 'If that's the way you want it . . .'

He knew what Max would be thinking, probably telling Jim Robinson or someone, that Shane had had it all going for him, he could have made the Olympics, because that was Max's great dream, to prove that his son could make something of his life – take on the world and win, would probably be how he expressed it. It was a damned shame. And if Danny's name came into it, as it probably would, then . . . Maybe he would even say that Danny was right, and that it should have been him and not Shane who was badly hurt. And maybe . . . Lying back with his eyes closed, Danny tortured himself by imagining the possible scenario. He tried to imagine how the conversation between Max and Jim Robinson would go – and knowing Max as well as he did, and Jim Robinson too, he didn't think he could be too far wrong.

So what have you got against Danny? Jim Robinson would ask, and if Max said he had nothing against Danny, Jim Robinson would say, rubbish, a man would have to be blind not to see the way he lived for Shane, and it *had* to be something more than the fact that he might have won a gold medal at the Olympics. Danny was a bit wild, sure, they both knew that, but that didn't explain what Max had against him . . .

And what *did* Max have against him? Danny had wondered about that often enough in the past – and now Max *did* have a reason. Danny knew Jim Robinson would stick up for him, try to make Max see reason, because Jim had always been there when Danny had a problem to unload. He had always listened to Danny. In many ways he had been more a father to Danny than Max had been, even if he did have four kids of his own and no wife to help him bring them up because she had died years ago.

In the meantime, Danny had some visitors. One or two of the kids from school popped in to see him and after only a matter of minutes began to show signs of restlessness and made excuses to leave. Danny was relieved to see them go; his heart wasn't in making small talk which became increasingly more of a strain. It was a little better when Scott Robinson came to visit him; they had much more in common, and the bad feelings over Kim had passed. Then, on another day, to his amazement, he had a visit from Shane.

'Hi, Squirt,' Shane cheerfully greeted him as the nurse wheeled his chair into the room. Danny could only stare at him; all sorts of things were happening inside him. 'So how are you feeling?' Shane asked after the nurse had gone.

Danny's lips were trembling. 'I'm sorry, Shane,' he whispered. 'It was all my fault.'

Shane was grinning at him. The wheelchair had been lined up at the side of the bed. 'Rubbish. It was the creep who robbed the bank. How could it be *your* fault?'

'If I hadn't made you drive to the beach that day . . .'

'Come off it, will you.' Shane placed his hand on Danny's arm. 'Honestly, you're carrying on like an old woman. And here I was, thinking maybe you could help me.'

'Help you?' Danny looked at him. Shane was still grinning. 'How?'

'I need to get away for a while,' Shane told him. 'I need time to sort myself out.' His grin faded to a reflective smile. 'You know, for a while there I thought I was going to spend the rest of my life flat on my back. That's a big thing to have to come to accept, and then, when I found I could move my hands, then my legs, and all the feeling started coming back again . . .' He laughed. 'Anyway, it didn't turn out to be as bad as everyone thought it would, and that's the main thing.' His face clouded briefly. 'It still means I can't do any more diving, though, and that's a big disappointment to Dad. But there are plenty of other things I can do,' he said brightening. 'It's not the end of the world.'

Danny was beginning to feel a little better now that he knew Shane wasn't holding it against him. He had even asked Danny to help him. 'How do you mean – help you?' he asked.

'By coming away with me.'

'What?'

'I thought we could take off somewhere – just the two of us. Go camping somewhere.'

Danny could hardly believe it. 'You mean . . . you and me?'

'Why not you and me?'

Danny was feeling better all the time. He was

beginning to have a very warm feeling inside him. 'Yeah ... sure, that would be great.'

Shane pushed his chair away from the bed. 'Okay then, that's decided. Now we have to decide where to go. Where do *you* think?'

'I don't know,' Danny said happily. 'You decide.' Anywhere Shane wanted would be fine with him.

4

Jim Robinson was climbing down the ladder from the roof of his house where he had been replacing some tiles when he first saw Anna. He was immediately struck by her dark and rather sultry attractiveness which reminded him of someone he either knew or had seen somewhere before.

She was in the yard of the Ramsay house next door. From his vantage point on the ladder, Jim watched her as she knocked again on the back door and then, when there was no response, peered in through the kitchen window. 'Hello there,' he called. 'Can I help you?'

She watched him as he descended the ladder and crossed to the fence. And then it came to him where he had seen her before – well, not exactly seen her before, not in the flesh, but he knew who she was. 'You're Anna, aren't you?' The resemblance was unmistakable; of course it was Maria Ramsay's sister; he had seen photographs of her.

She looked surprised. 'Yes . . . yes, I am.'

'I'm Jim Robinson.' He gestured towards the house behind him. 'I live here.'

'Ah.' Her face lit up in recognition. 'So *you're* Jim Robinson. I've heard so much about you.'

Jim had heard a lot about her, too. They shook hands over the fence. 'Max is out on a job, but Maria should be back shortly.'

'I see. And the boys? How are the boys?'

She really was very attractive, Jim thought. The photographs he had seen of her had no more than hinted at how lovely she was. Her eyes were large and luminous; her skin was flawless. 'They're going to be fine,' he told her.

'I was very worried when Maria told me about the accident,' Anna explained. 'I came down as fast as I could.'

'Yes, I'm sure you did.'

'Yes. I should have phoned with the flight details, but I'm afraid I overlooked it in my rush to get here.' Her voice was vibrant and a little husky. 'Look,' Jim suggested, 'there's no point waiting out here until they get back, so why don't you come and wait at our place until they do?'

'Well . . .' She studied him thoughtfully for a moment. 'If you're sure it's not inconvenient.'

'Of course not.' He opened the gate in the fence. Anna stepped through into the Robinson back yard.

'You recognised me then,' she said.

'From photographs.'

'Ah...'

'But none of them do you justice.'

'Thank you,' she said with a light, silvery laugh.

It was late in the afternoon; in an hour or so it would be dark. In the kitchen, Helen was preparing Lucy's dinner. Scott volunteered to watch out for Maria. 'Sorry we have to entertain in the kitchen,' Helen told Anna, 'but Lucy always watches TV at this time, and I have to keep an eye on the dinner.'

'The kitchen is always the nicest part of the house, anyway,' Anna said pleasantly. 'At least, I think so.'

'I think so, too,' Helen said. 'Perhaps it's because we have to spend so much time in it.'

Jim smiled. Bless you, Helen, he thought. He didn't know what he would do without her. Since Anne had died she had been worth her weight in gold, stepping in without a moment's hesitation to take over the day to day running of the house and to look after her daughter's children.

'Danny and Shane will be pleased to see you,' he said.

Anna smiled and sipped the coffee Helen had made for her. 'I suppose Danny has grown quite a lot by now. It's been nearly two years since I saw him, and Maria and Max didn't bring the boys when they came up to Queensland for mother's funeral.'

Jim nodded. Maria had told him that her sister had nursed their mother during her sickness; she hadn't wanted her mother to spend what little time she had left in a hospital, among strangers.

Scott appeared in the doorway. 'Maria's home,' he announced, and Jim felt a little disappointed that Anna would now be leaving them.

'I hope we'll see some more of you,' Helen said as Anna finished her coffee and stood up.

Anna smiled. It was such a dazzling smile – and it was directed straight at Jim who, in its warmth and candour, suddenly felt like a fumbling, awkward, lovestruck kid again. 'She's very attractive, isn't she?' Helen observed after Anna, escorted by Scott, had left the house – and Jim could only say amen to that.

Later that same evening, before dinner, he saw her again when he was having a beer with Max in Max's house. Jim had been concerned by Max's attitude towards Danny. Max had been quite bitter about what had happened; he had railed against Danny, and Jim had defended him, saying that he was a good kid, a bit restless maybe – but what kid wasn't at that age? Now, tonight, Max told him to forget what he had said about Danny the other night, and Jim guessed he realised how unfair he had been to the kid. 'The problem is,' Jim said with a chuckle, 'when you come right down to it, he's a chip off the old block. You're a bit too much alike.'

But even as he said this, he could see that Max didn't really want to discuss it any more. Then Maria and Anna came into the room. They had been to the hospital to see the boys, and reported that everything was fine with them. Danny had got over his depression, Maria said; Shane had had a talk to him, and now the two of them were eagerly making arrangements to go on a camping trip together, which was good news.

Conscious that Anna was watching him, Jim rose to his feet. 'I'd better get a move on,' he said.

'You haven't finished your beer,' Max pointed out.

'Why don't you stay and eat with us?' Maria suggested brightly.

The invitation was endorsed by Max. 'Yeah, and I'll open a bottle of red. We've got something to celebrate now that Anna's here.'

'And now we know that both the boys are going to be all right,' Maria said chirpily. Her eyes were bright; she was obviously very happy.

Jim was still hesitant. 'Well, look, I'd love to, but my life wouldn't be worth living if I upset the family routine,' he demurred.

'Maria won't let me open the red if you're not here,' Max said.

'That's right,' Maria agreed.

They were insistent, and in the end Jim, whose refusal had been half-hearted anyway because he really would have welcomed the opportunity to be in Anna's company, agreed to stay on for dinner. He noted with a flush of pleasure how pleased Anna in particular was by his acceptance.

And by the end of that evening, Jim Robinson knew as certainly as he could know anything, that he was falling in love with Anna.

Love – it was a marvellous feeling. It had happened to him only once before, and now Anne was dead, she had died far too young and he still grieved for her. But now, with Anna, he realised that while his love for her could never truly replace that he had felt for Anne – and it struck him in a moment of fancy that there might have been more than just coincidence in the similarity of their names – it could coexist with that earlier love, combining with it to strengthen him and make him feel whole again. It made him feel young once more, and carefree. And it wasn't long before he realised she was beginning to feel the same way about him.

It seemed that during the days that followed they were hardly out of each other's company. They went out for dinner at small, intimate restaurants; they visited the markets where Jim bought her flowers; they went for ferry rides and walks in the park where they fed the ducks with crusts of bread. They laughed a lot, and Jim told her about himself, and the kids, and about Helen who had been such a tower of strength since she had moved into the house after the death of Jim's wife, her daughter. In Anna's company, Jim felt like a kid again; all the years had been stripped away. Yes, he was quite convinced he was in love with her. He was happier than he had been in years, certainly since Anne had been alive, and it wasn't long before he began to have thoughts of marrying Anna. She would be an ideal wife – he was quite convinced of it. She would fit in very nicely with the family, he thought, and if Julie was showing every sign of coolness towards her, that couldn't be helped, she would just have to learn to adjust.

Perhaps it was understandable that Julie should be cool towards Anna. As Jim's oldest daughter, she had been taking on more responsibility in the household, as much as her job in the bank permitted, and obviously she saw Anna as a potential rival who would take on herself those responsibilities if she became Jim's wife. Julie's role as homemaker which she fulfilled quite happily in conjunction with her grandmother, would be usurped, and Julie would regard this as a defeat. She was not the sort of girl who would easily accept that. She was headstrong and impulsive; she tended to take over. Jim was a little worried by her attitude towards Anna.

But Julie was the only one of his family he

needed to worry about. Helen was very taken with Anna, as were the two boys, Paul and Scott. Lucy might have had her own ideas, but then, at 10 years of age, she could be talked to and easily persuaded that what happened – *if* it happened, Jim had to remind himself – would be for the best.

Yet, on the night Anna came to the Robinsons for dinner, Jim could see there was something on Lucy's mind. She kept looking reflectively at her grandmother and at one stage sat beside her and gave her an impulsive hug. 'You're not mad at me, are you, Gran?' she asked.

'Of course not, darling.' Helen was clearly a little puzzled by the question.

'And if I try to be good, you won't go away, will you?'

'What on earth are you talking about, darling?' Helen queried, and Jim noticed that Julie was suddenly looking uncomfortable. He wondered what she had been saying to Lucy. It could even be that she had suggested to her that their grandmother might have to go away if Anna moved in which, of course, was utter rubbish.

'Julie said that...'

Julie quickly broke in. 'Lucy thought you were angry with her for getting her dress dirty, that's all.'

Anna and Jim exchanged a quick glance. Anna was looking particularly beautiful that night; she had done something different with her hair which looked lustrous under the dining room light.

Helen had done most of the cooking. Anna had brought a cake which she had baked herself. Everyone thought the cake was delicious, especially Scott, and this somehow seemed to annoy Julie who said, drily, 'Oh, honestly, he'll eat *anything* you put in front of him, as long as it's food.'

'Thank you, Julie,' Helen said with a smile. 'As head cook and bottle washer of this family I think that's a very nice compliment.'

Jim watched Julie warily; he knew she had been having a dig at Anna. If Anna herself realised, she wasn't showing it.

The Ramsay boys had gone camping after their discharge from the hospital. Anna had allowed Maria to talk her into staying on for a while, and Jim was glad she had, although he knew it wouldn't be for much longer.

Julie turned to Anna. 'I expect you'll be glad to get back to Queensland for a bit of peace and quiet,' she remarked pleasantly enough.

Anna's smile faltered; she looked suddenly undecided. 'I don't think Anna's in too much of a hurry,' Jim said quickly.

'I certainly hope not,' Helen said, then smiled at Anna. 'It's such a shame you have to live so far away.'

'Yes . . .' With a twinge of pleasure, Jim saw the

fondness in her eyes as she directed another quick glance at him. It was as if she were willing him to reply for her. 'I *would* like to be nearer,' she murmured.

Then Paul was suggesting that if it was a fine day tomorrow, why didn't they all go to the beach, and Julie rather crisply reminded him that tomorrow was Sunday, and on Sundays she cooked a roast for the family's midday meal, as he well knew. Paul said he was sick of roast every Sunday, and Helen suggested that they could have it in the evening instead.

'Anna and I have made other plans, anyway,' Jim told them. Tomorrow was the day they had arranged to go to the markets. Julia gave him a stony look. Jim knew she was disappointed, but they had made their plans, and she would have to accept that.

'I want to stay with Gran,' Lucy said possessively.

'You will, you will,' Helen said, giving her a hug.

When the table was cleared, Anna offered to help with the washing up. 'Dad usually does that for me,' Lucy said tightly.

They were in the kitchen. Jim could hear them from the other room as he sipped his coffee. 'Well, why don't you give him the night off?' Anna suggested.

'I don't think he'd like that,' Julie replied. 'You

see, we always give Gran a rest on Saturday night, and again on Sunday after we've had the roast. No, we enjoy it. It's about our only chance to get together and talk about things.'

'I see,' Anna said thoughtfully.

Julie went on. 'You see, after Mum died, I guess I just... sort of stepped in. And I think it helped Dad an awful lot that things didn't change too much. Because they were terrifically close. So... I think it's best if you leave things the way they are. The washing up, I mean.'

Listening to her, Jim knew that he had been right, and that Julie *did* resent Anna. Jim had heard enough. He stood up and moved to the kitchen door. 'Anna, why don't you come back here into the other room and relax,' he said, fixing Julie with a cold stare. 'Paul can help Julie with the washing up when he's ready.' He could tell by Julie's expression that she was hurt, but that couldn't be helped, she would get over it sooner or later – she *had* to get over it sooner or later, and the sooner she did, the better.

The following morning, on his way to pick up Anna from next door, he asked Helen what she thought of her.

'I like her very much,' Helen told him.

'So do I.'

'So I've noticed,' Helen said with a chuckle.

There was still something Jim wanted to know. It was important for him to know. Anne had been her daughter, and she had done so much for him and the family after Anne's death. He owed her every consideration.

'It doesn't upset you, does it, that I'm seeing so much of her?'

'Of course not,' Helen assured him gently. 'The only way I would be upset would be if you threw away a chance to be happy.'

He knew it was what she would say; he had just wanted to hear her say it. 'Thanks, Helen,' he said warmly, giving her a kiss before he turned away to the gate.

It was a bright, sunny day, and their spirits were perfectly attuned to it. With Anna holding his arm, they strolled through the crowded markets. Anna bought a water melon, and a straw hat which she laughingly placed on Jim's head. They looked at pot plants and junk jewellery. They ate ice-cream and oranges. Jim put the straw hat on her head and took a photograph of her. He told her she looked beautiful – even in a straw hat.

'It's been great fun, Jim,' Anna said later when they were having a cup of coffee.

'And it's just the beginning,' Jim said happily. 'I have a long, long list of wonderful things I have planned for us to do.'

Anna suddenly became more serious. 'I'm afraid I'm not going to be here for much longer,' she said quietly.

The straw hat and the water melon were on the empty chair beside Jim. They had been served their coffee; Anna was thoughtfully stirring hers. Jim laughed.

'I was hoping you might extend your stay – for thirty years or so.'

'That's rather difficult, Jim.'

Jim leaned forward on his chair. 'Anna, I'm in love with you,' he said in a low, intense voice. 'You must know that.'

Anna stopped stirring her coffee and looked up at him across the table. 'Jim, I'm afraid there already *is* someone in my life,' she said faintly. 'That's why I have to go back.' She sighed. Jim felt as if he had just been struck a savage blow. 'That's why I have to go back,' Anna continued. 'He's a good man, and... and I just can't walk away.' She shook her head. 'I'm sorry, Jim. There's no future for us.'

Jim stared at her, trying to convince himself that he hadn't heard what she had just told him, that he had got it mixed up somehow. But he knew he hadn't got it mixed up, that there was no point in trying to delude himself. 'It never occurred to me there might be another man,' he said in a small voice.

'All of this happened so quickly,' Anna told him. And it had – just a few days, but Jim had come to believe that he knew just about everything there was to know about her. Now he realised he knew practically nothing. 'He's such a kind man. And he's been very patient.'

'Do you love him?'

She didn't answer him. Her eyes were turned to the window. 'Anna?'

'Please, Jim.'

'I have to know. Are you going back because you love him?'

Her eyes swung back to his. Her gaze was direct. 'I'm going back because I'm frightened of the way I feel about you,' she said.

They drove back to Ramsay Street in silence. 'I do wish you would change your mind,' Jim said when he had stopped the car outside his house. 'Please . . .'

He studied her earnestly. 'Since Anne died,' he said, 'I haven't even looked at another woman. And then you came along.' He gave a nervous laugh. 'Oh, I know a lot of people would laugh at the idea of a bloke my age talking about love at first sight, but . . . I don't know, it was as if I had waited all these years for someone like you to come along. And . . . and I had hoped you felt the same.'

There were tears in Anna's eyes. 'I did,' she whispered. 'I still do.'

'Oh, Anna.'

Moving closer to her, he took her in his arms and kissed her. For a moment she was unyielding, then returned his kiss with an ardour that quite matched his own.

At Jim's insistence, Anna had dinner once again at the Robinsons that evening. Tonight, there was only cold meat from Julie's Sunday roast, and salad. As she was helping herself to the potato salad, Anna remarked on the diamond and ruby ring she had noticed for the first time on Helen's finger. 'It was my mother's,' Helen told her.

About half-way through the meal, Lucy dropped her serviette. At the same moment both she and Anna bent to pick it up from the floor. Their heads bumped.

'Oh, I'm sorry, Lucy.' Anna's hand reached out to touch Lucy's head where she had bumped it.

'Don't!' Lucy cried, scrambled off her chair. 'Get off!' She ran out of the room.

Jim stood up and prepared to go after her. 'She'll be back when she's hungry,' Helen said, motioning him to sit down again.

Jim sat down and, reaching for Anna's hand, squeezed it reassuringly. He would have a word with Lucy later.

Before she left that night, when she collected her bag from Helen's room, Anna ran into Helen and Lucy in the corridor. Helen told her she was just putting Lucy to bed, and would say goodnight now rather than come outside to see her off.

Anna thanked her and said goodnight. Lucy didn't respond when Anna said goodnight to her.

Jim offered to walk her home, but she told him not to bother. They kissed, and she said, 'Until tomorrow then.' Jim told her he could hardly wait until tomorrow, and Anna laughed and said that was too bad.

Jim was having a cup of coffee Julie had made for him when Helen came into the living room. She looked worried. 'Jim, have you seen my ring lying around?' she asked.

'No. No, I haven't.'

'That's funny,' Helen said with a perplexed frown. 'I took it off in my bedroom when I was with Lucy. And now I can't find it.'

Then Lucy came running into the room. 'Anna took it,' she cried.

'What?' Helen swung on her.

'Well, she was admiring it,' Julie reminded her.

'Don't be ridiculous Julie.' Jim snapped. It was just too stupid for words to think that Anna...

'Anna took it.' Lucy was shrill and insistent. 'I saw her.'

'Go to your room Lucy,' Helen commanded.

Lucy left. Julie followed her. Jim was smouldering. *Something* was going on, and he was determined to get to the bottom of it.

The following morning, at breakfast, after Lucy had been packed off by Helen to clean her teeth so as not to be late for school, Jim asked her if she had found her ring. Helen gave him a knowing smile. 'Of course,' he said. 'I know where Lucy hides her special treasures.'

So Lucy had taken the ring herself. Jim had suspected as much. He rounded on Julie. 'I want an apology from you,' he demanded gruffly.

Julie put down her cup. She was in her bank uniform. 'I didn't actually say anyone had actually stolen the ring,' she said defensively.

'Don't split hairs with me, Julie,' Jim grated. 'I hope you're proud of the way you've mixed Lucy up.'

Julie stood up. 'I'd better get to work,' she muttered uncomfortably.

Jim nodded. 'All right then – but you and I have got some talking to do when you get home.'

In the Ramsay house, Anna led Jim into the living room. Maria was busy in the kitchen; Max was off on a job somewhere. 'It's too early to talk of marriage,' Anna said. 'I mean, your family . . . I need to get to know them better.'

'If you're thinking of Lucy,' Jim said, 'she's just confused. Normally she's a good kid. I'm sure she'll grow to love you.'

It might take Julie longer to accept Anna, but Jim was quite sure she would – in time. 'There's also Max to consider,' Anna told him.

'Max? What's it got to do with him?'

'He's been like a brother to me, Jim,' Anna said quietly. 'It wasn't easy for us when we first came

55

to this country. Max was marvellous. He even taught my father to speak English.'

'Yes.' Jim remembered something Maria had told him about Max and her family. 'They worked together, didn't they?'

'That's right. Dad was a tiler, and Max had just started out as a plumber.' She smiled faintly. Jim could hear Maria moving about in the kitchen. 'You know, a lot of people just don't understand Max. They think he's the type of Aussie who would run a mile from a family like ours – especially in those days. You know what it was like with foreigners. But Max took it all in his stride – the language problems, the different backgrounds. He loved my father.'

Jim knew what Max was like; they had been mates for years. Anna went on, a little wistfully. 'They were working together on the day of the accident. After my father was killed, Max just took over. He worked at two jobs so he could look after us, Maria and I, to give us a home and a proper education.'

Jim hadn't known that, but he wasn't surprised, Max being the type of guy he was. Then Anna mentioned that person in her life she had referred to in the coffee shop. 'Gino's been the same,' she said. She touched his arm, her eyes sought his understanding. 'If you only knew him ... how good he was when my Mum was alive.'

There was not much Jim could say to that except to tell her that he loved her. 'I still want to marry you,' he said intensely.

'Oh, Jim...' Her eyes, warm and melting, told him everything.

A few nights later, when Jim brought Anna home after having taken her out to dinner and a show, Max was waiting for them in his living room, even though it was already after midnight. The television was on. Max had a can of beer in his hand. 'I thought you would be in bed,' Jim remarked.

'No.' Max stood up and, crossing to the television, switched it off. 'I wanted to talk to the both of you.' He sounded very serious. 'All right,' he said, turning back to them. 'I won't beat about the bush. I'll come straight to the point. I think both of you are making one hell of a mistake.'

'Anything else?' Jim asked tensely.

'Yep.' Max's expression was stern. 'I think Anna should go back to Queensland as soon as possible.'

Jim looked at Anna. 'What have you got against Jim?' Anna wanted to know.

'It's not Jim,' Max replied gruffly. 'It's the whole flaming mess you'll both end up in.'

It had been an enjoyable night for Jim and Anna. Now it was turning sour. 'Why don't you spell it out for us, Max?' Jim demanded.

'All right.' Max nodded. 'Well, for starters,

you're expecting her to take over the running of four kids. And two of them hate her guts.'

That was too much. 'They *don't* hate her guts!' Jim exclaimed. 'And anyway, whatever they feel, they'll soon get over it.'

Max snorted. 'Yeah? You really think so, do you? And what if they don't? Look, mate,' Max continued reasonably, 'let's face it, you hardly know Anna. You don't know what she's like.' Anna was looking down at the floor. 'She's led a very sheltered life up there in Queensland, looking after her mother until she died.'

'I don't see what difference that makes,' Jim muttered.

'Every difference in the world, mate.' Max nodded to Anna who was clearly embarrassed at being discussed so openly. 'She's like a daughter to me – always has been.' His voice lost its rough edge as he addressed Anna. 'So just go home, Anna. You've got a nice uncomplicated life up there with a man who's got no family problems. He's even building a home for you.' Max sat down again in the armchair. 'I'm sorry, Jim, but the longer things are left unsaid, the worse they're going to be.'

Maria came into the room in her dressing gown. 'What's wrong?' she asked, looking at each of them with a worried frown.

Jim pointed to Max. 'He's wrong,' he said angrily. He stood over Max. 'So you just keep out of our lives, Max,' he growled, 'because whether you or any of my family like it or not, Anna and I are going to be married.'

So it was out then. The announcement had been made, although certainly not in the circumstances any of them expected, least of all Jim. Max had stated his objections, but they had been overruled. He would just have to accept the situation.

Maria, on the other hand, was excited by the prospect of her sister's marriage to Jim; she made no bones about telling Jim this. What was more, she set about making arrangements for a party to celebrate the engagement with great enthusiasm, whether Max liked it or not.

Jim hoped his family would turn up for the party. Paul and Scott were enthusiastic, and when he suggested to Julie that she might give Maria a call to see if there was anything she could do to help, Julie said rather sullenly that she was sure Maria would be able to manage quite well without her. Jim was disappointed by her reaction.

But for Anna, once she had thought about it – and seeing the rift Jim's announcement was causing between Max and Maria – it seemed it was all happening too quickly, and she didn't know if she could cope with it. Then, too, there was Julie's negative attitude towards her. Jim told her not to worry about those things, that what they were doing was right; their own happiness was all that mattered. Then he took a small velvet box from his pocket and, opening it, showed her the diamond engagement ring he had bought for her, and which he had intended to present to her that night at the party, but because she was so worried, because she was having these doubts, he decided to give it to her now. As he slipped it on her finger, Anna's doubts appeared to vanish.

At the party, to which most of the neighbours had been invited, Jim asked Max if he would be best man at the wedding, which to him seemed only right because he had been best man at Max's wedding. Max was startled. 'What? Have you already named the day?'

'No, but we're still asking you.'

The house was full of people. There was plenty to eat and drink. Max shook his head. 'I'm sorry, Jim,' he said. 'I can't do it.'

Jim was about to protest when Maria joined them and asked how it was all going. When Jim told her that Max had refused to be his best man, she gave Max a murderous look, and would have remonstrated with him if Paul hadn't called for silence just then, cleared his throat and said, looking at his father and Anna who were standing together, 'On behalf of everyone here tonight I'd just like to say that we're happy for you, Dad, and Anna.' He smiled at Anna and raised his glass. 'And welcome to the Robinson family.'

This was greeted with applause, and murmurs of 'hear, hear'. Jim was touched. Anna smiled radiantly as Paul handed her a parcel and a card in an envelope. Jim glanced across at Julie who, he noted, was looking quite sour in the midst of the general merriment.

Flushed with pleasure, Anna was opening the envelope. 'We all signed it,' Paul told her. 'Even Lucy.'

'Thanks, son,' Jim said. He nodded in the direction of the parcel. 'What is it?'

But before Paul could reply, Julie broke in with the tart comment, 'Well, I wouldn't know. It wasn't my idea.' She moved away as Max demanded that everyone charge their glasses for the toast he proposed to make. Jim knew he wasn't happy about making it, and that Maria had persuaded him into it. He kept it short and simple. 'To Anna and Jim,' he said, holding up his own glass. 'Congratulations.'

'And every happiness,' Maria added.

Then everybody sang 'For they are jolly good fellows'.

Food was passed around, glasses were replenished. Helen came up to Anna and handed her a small box. 'I wanted to give you this,' she said warmly. 'Something personal from me to you.'

Anna lifted the lid of the box to reveal an antique brooch of beaten silver and amethyst. 'It's beautiful,' she gasped. 'Oh, Maria, come and look at this.'

When Julie saw the brooch, her face darkened. 'You can't give her that,' she snapped. 'That was my mother's.'

'It belonged to *my* mother, Julie,' her grandmother crisply reminded her, 'and I shall give it to anyone I please.'

Julie was upset. She glared at Anna. 'You . . . you're taking *everything* away from this family,' she cried. 'I hope you're satisfied.' She raised her hand and before Jim could stop her, she slapped Anna's face.

The room was suddenly silent as people turned to see what was happening. Julie ran out of the room. Furious, Jim started after her, but Anna grabbed his arm. 'Jim please,' she urged breathlessly. 'Don't go.'

He didn't have a chance to confront his daughter with what she had done until later that evening when, after the party had broken up, he found her in the kitchen of their own house. She was boiling water for a cup of coffee. Jim was still furious with her. She had done something quite unforgivable.

'I never hit you in your life before,' he said, striving to keep his voice level. 'But I came so close to it back there, believe you me. Now I want you to go back next door and apologise to her.'

She had her back to him. She shook her head. 'No,' she said almost inaudibly. 'I can't do that,

Dad.'

'I see.' She was still being defiant, and it was time for the ultimatum he had made up his mind to deliver if she persisted in her attitude. 'Well, let me tell you this, Julie. I'm going to marry Anna, like it or not, and unless you see your way clear to apologising to her and stop behaving like a child, I want you to move out of the house. And the sooner, the better.'

He could see that she was stunned by his ultimatum, but he wasn't prepared to argue with her; his mind was made up. He left her alone to think it over.

The next day, he met Anna in the park beside the lake. She had called him at his office and told him she wanted to see him. She looked unhappy.

'It isn't Julie's fault, you know,' she said after he had told her he wanted her to apologise for the incident at the party. 'I mean, look at the way Max is carrying on. And . . .' she made a small gesture of helplessness . . . 'it just seems to me that any happiness between us is doomed.'

'Hey, hey.' She needed to be encouraged; this wasn't what Jim wanted to hear at all. 'That's enough of that. Look,' he went on cheerfully, 'I've been thinking. We're not spending enough time alone together, so why don't we go out for dinner tonight? And we won't talk about anyone. Not Julie or Max. It'll be just the two of us.'

'All right,' Anna said, but she was still

uncertain. 'But let me say this. If I am to be the cause of any more problems between you and Julie, I won't be able to cope.' Her smile was a little shaky. 'Max was right. I *have* led a very sheltered life up north. But the last thing on earth I want to do is destroy a family – especially your family.'

Jim was still a little concerned about Helen, despite her repeated assurances that she would be all right, that she had planned a very happy future for herself once Jim and Anna were married. 'I'll only be moving into a flat,' she told him, 'not out of your lives.'

'Well, as long as you're sure that's what you want to do,' Jim said doubtfully. He didn't want her to think she was under an obligation to move.

'Positive.' Helen was setting the table for dinner. 'Anyway, you don't want an old hen fussing around when you and Anna are starting out on married life.'

'It's just that we owe you such a lot,' Jim said. 'When Anne died, it seemed the most natural thing in the world for you to move in and help me bring up the kids. It was only later that I realised what a sacrifice you had made for us.'

'Oh, sacrifice, nothing.' Helen moved out into the kitchen. 'It gave me a new lease of life – just as marrying Anna will give *you* a new lease of life.'

Jim followed her into the kitchen. 'Do you really think it will work out?' he asked.

'If you want it to,' she replied, 'it will.'

But there was still the worry about Julie. 'You know, I meant it when I told Julie she either had to apologise to Anna or move out of the house.'

Helen gave him a long and level look. 'And that's quite fair enough,' she said simply.

As Jim told Anna later, when they were having a pre-dinner drink at the Ramsay's, his mother-in-law was about the wisest person he knew, and Anna couldn't have agreed with him more.

'And she's right when she says that the sooner we're married, the better,' Jim remarked.

Then Anna remembered something. 'Oh, I almost forgot. The photos.'

They had taken a lot of photographs on the occasions when they had been out together. Anna opened her bag. 'They're really very good,' she said.

As she took the photographs from her bag, she dropped them. Jim reached forward to pick them up from the floor and as he did so, he noticed an envelope that had fallen with them. It was addressed, and stamped. He picked up the letter. He recognised the name on the envelope, and the Queensland address. 'Oh, I see you haven't told Gino then,' he observed.

'Not yet,' she replied quickly. She held her hand out for the letter. He passed it to her. 'I'll post it in the morning.'

The subject of Gino was brought up again

when Max arrived home from work. There was still a coolness between him and Jim. 'Have you told Gino yet?' he asked Anna.

'No . . .'

'She's written him a letter,' Jim supplied.

Anna appeared to be a little nervous. 'I haven't posted it . . .'

Max had helped himself to a beer from the refrigerator. 'Well, listen,' he said shortly, 'if you two are going to go ahead with this thing . . . don't you think he ought to know?'

Jim was becoming annoyed with Max; he was really making such a great issue of this thing. 'Lay off, Max, will you,' he snapped.

'And I'm not going to post it,' Anna said softly.

Jim gaped at her. 'Anna?'

'I'm going to tell him in person,' she said. 'I owe him that much at least.'

That meant going back to Queensland. Jim didn't think he could bear to be parted from her even for the time it took her to travel up to Queensland, tell Gino what she had to tell him, and then come back again. But Gino had to be told, and if that was the way she preferred to do it, well, fair enough. Later, in the restaurant where he took her that night for dinner, and where, after they had eaten, they sat in their alcove sipping champagne, it seemed to him that she was rather subdued. He put it down to the prospect of having to face Gino. He was feeling fairly subdued himself; there was quite a lot on his mind.

Anna smiled at him across the table. 'You know, you remind me of a neighbour of ours in Queensland. He never smiled. But his wife, on the other hand, was a very happy woman. She would say that it was her being so happy that kept him going. You've been looking like that man all evening.'

'I'm sorry.' Jim smiled back at her. She was right; he wasn't being very stimulating company tonight. 'I suppose it's having so many sad faces around me. It must be catching.'

'And it shouldn't be a time for sadness, should it?'

No, not a time for sadness. 'I know we've got a few problems,' he said soberly, 'but it won't be for much longer. You know what Max is like. He'll come round before long, and give us his blessing.' He took the bottle from the bucket beside him and refilled her glass. 'Helen says she's looking forward to doing other things with her life – and the boys are delighted that we're getting married. And it's really only a matter of time . . .'

'What about Julie?' Anna interrupted.

Julie . . . It wasn't so easy with Julie. 'I know you don't want her to move out of the house, but I think it's best if she does.'

'No, Jim.' She laid her hand on his. 'Talk to

her. Ask her to stay.'

'No.' He said it so vehemently that people looked across at them from the nearer tables. He lowered his voice. 'She slapped your face. I can't forgive her for that.'

'Yes...' Anna seemed to be lost in thought for a long moment. She looked up at him. 'That slap did something to me,' she said sadly. 'It brought me to my senses.' Her hand was still resting on his. She regarded him sorrowfully. 'We've been living in a fool's paradise, you and I. I've been preparing myself to say this all evening, and it's not easy, because I do love you...'

'And I love you,' Jim said fervently.

'And I'm saying goodbye. I'm going home, and I'm not coming back.'

Perhaps he had sensed it all along. There had been something weighing pretty heavily on her mind all evening. He suddenly felt cold inside. 'I just wish I could avoid hurting you like this,' Anna went on, 'but we both know that this is the way it's got to be. You won't see me again; I'm flying home first thing in the morning and... and... I'll never be sorry we met.' She stood up, and coming around the table, leaned over him and kissed his cheek. Her eyes were glistening. 'Goodbye, Jim,' she whispered, then gathering herself, walked quickly out of the restaurant.

5

Daphne Lawrence opened the door wearing only her tights and a leotard. She had been working on a new dance routine when the doorbell sounded.

'Does Desmond Clarke live here?' The woman was middle-aged. There was a suitcase on the step beside her.

'Desmond? Oh, you mean Des. Yes he does.'

'Oh, good. Then I've got the right place.' It seemed to Daphne that this woman who she had never seen before was making a shrewd appraisal of her. 'Is he home?'

It was eleven thirty in the morning, and Des was at the bank. 'No, I'm sorry, he's out.'

'That's all right.' The woman picked up the suitcase. 'I'll just come in and wait.'

Daphne was puzzled; Des hadn't told her he was expecting anyone – and there did seem to be a sense of purpose about this woman. 'He'll be at the bank,' Daphne told her. 'You can call him there.'

'Oh no,' the woman said, moving past Daphne into the hall. 'I'm here to stay.' Daphne could only stare at her. What *was* this? 'You see I'm his mother.'

Oh my God, Daphne thought, following the woman into the living room. Des's mother was supposed to be back in Perth. He hardly ever talked about her, and when he did it was in such a way as to suggest that Perth, with the breadth of the whole continent between them, was where he was quite happy for her to be. Daphne didn't think he would be pleased now that his mother had suddenly taken it into her head to drop in on him out of the blue.

And now the woman, having put her suitcase down again, was beaming at her, advancing towards her with her arms outstretched. 'And you're exactly the way I imagined you... Lorraine,' she said joyfully as she took Daphne in her arms and gave her a tight hug that almost took Daphne's breath away.

Daphne was dismayed. She had to tell this woman she had the wrong girl, that she wasn't Lorraine who had pulled out of the wedding at the last moment and had come and taken all her furniture away. It was going to be hard to explain to her – but she had to do the best she could, standing there in her tights and leotard. She had to explain that she was renting a room in the house and that everything was above board, and if she did most of the cooking and the housework, the washing and ironing, and sewed buttons on Des's shirts, that didn't mean there was anything more between them than that, no matter what people thought. And they were thinking all sorts of things, particularly that awful Brown woman across the street. But the place was home to her and she only wished, like any woman would, to make it as comfortable and cheerful as she could. Des appreciated that. Maybe he appreciated it too much. Maybe he was coming to depend on her more and more. But, heck, she didn't mind. The only trouble was that while Des was becoming more and more approving of her efforts around the place, he was also becoming possessive, and even jealous when she went out to work at night. He thought that a girl who took off her clothes as a professional had to be laying herself open to temptation every time she went out on an engagement, that it was somehow more than just a job, which was silly, because a job was all it was. She had a talent and she used it quite dispassionately. And an engagement was an engagement, and she always did the best she could, whether it was at a football or rowing club, or a private party, popping out of a cake – a hoary old routine, that one, but it still went down well – on someone's birthday. But she didn't tell all this to Des's mother from Perth; all she said was that she was a tenant. Des could tell her what he liked when he arrived home. They had arranged to go out for dinner that night. Daphne wasn't so sure now if they could go, now that Des's mother was here.

Of course it was a huge shock to Des when he came home that evening to find his mother already installed in the spare room. 'What the hell are you doing here, Mum?' was his greeting.

'Well, that's a nice way to greet me after flying all the way from Perth.'

'You might have given me some warning.'

'You might have told me you weren't married. I... thought she was Lorraine. I was so embarrassed.'

Daphne decided she didn't really like Mrs Clarke. There was something cloying about her, all sweetness and light on the surface, but something quite steely just below. When Des told her that he had intended to take Daphne out to dinner, but supposed now that she was here, he would have to cancel it, she insisted that they go, she didn't want to be in their way; the one thing she did not want to do was disrupt their life, so go on, she said, take your young lady out, go and have dinner and enjoy yourselves.

When they were ready to leave, Daphne asked her if she would be all right in the house by herself. Mrs Clarke replied that she thought she would manage quite well on her own. Then she became a little wistful. 'Mothers know when they're not wanted, Daphne,' she said. 'You'll find that out for yourself one of these days.'

Daphne wasn't sure what to say to that. 'I'd hardly say Des didn't *want* you. It's just that...'

Des finished it for her. 'It's just that Mum knows I live my own life now that I've grown up,' he said with a small, tight smile. 'Isn't that right, Mum?'

Mrs Clarke's own smile was bland. 'Now away you go, you two. Don't rush your dinner on my account. Just enjoy yourselves.'

They said goodnight and headed for the front door. They had almost reached it when, suddenly, there was a sharp cry behind them. Daphne turned back into the living room where Mrs Clarke was gasping and clutching her chest.

'Mrs Clarke,' Daphne cried. 'Are you all right?' Mrs Clarke was moaning. Her face was contorted with pain. 'Call the doctor,' Daphne ordered Des. 'It could be a heart attack.'

'Or indigestion,' Des remarked. He didn't sound too concerned.

'Water,' Mrs Clarke whispered. 'I need some water... please.'

Daphne turned to Des, who nodded and hurried into the kitchen. 'Sorry about dinner,' he said offhandedly and, as she tried to comfort the stricken woman, Daphne wondered why he was treating this so casually.

As it was, Mrs Clarke's attack was short-lived.

After some moments she claimed she was feeling much better. All she needed, she said, was one of her pills and she would be feeling one hundred per cent again. But for Des and Daphne, the evening was spoilt; there was no way they could go out now and leave her alone in the house.

It was inevitable that Mrs Clarke would find out the truth about Daphne sooner or later – and just as inevitable that she should be shocked to learn that her son was living in the same house as a woman who made a living by taking off her clothes. She learnt this from someone, possibly Julie Robinson from next door who had been going out with Des before Lorraine came along, and still held something of a grudge against him; or from Carol Brown across the street, who everyone knew had a bad drinking problem; or even from Max Ramsay who had never been reconciled to the fact that there was a *stripper* living in the street that bore his grandfather's name. Be that as it may, Mrs Clarke, who was quick to make friends in the neighbourhood, did find out about Daphne, and was appalled. And, of course, she lost no time in bringing it up with Des, whose reaction was, so what? Mrs Clarke was even more distressed by his seeming indifference.

When Daphne came into the living room that evening, Mrs Clarke was advancing on her son with a tape measure. 'I don't *need* a sweater,

Mum,' he protested, backing away from her.

'It will give me something to do,' she said in a hurt tone. 'It will while away the lonely hours.'

'There's no need to be lonely, Mum. Daphne's here most of the day.'

Mrs Clarke sniffed. 'That lady is not exactly my idea of company.' Then she saw Daphne in the doorway, and her face hardened. She moved to the door.

'Oh, don't leave on my account,' Daphne said with exaggerated sweetness. 'I'll be heading out to dinner soon.'

'I'm not feeling well,' Mrs Clarke said uncomfortably. 'Something must have brought on one of my little turns.' She hurried away.

Daphne switched off her smile. The more she saw of that woman the less she liked her. She had been making sly remarks, full of innuendo, to Daphne all day. 'How do you put up with it?' she asked Des.

He shrugged. He seemed relieved that his mother had gone. 'Now you know why I left Perth. But she's just here on a holiday. She won't stay long.'

'And that's exactly how she gets away with it,' Daphne said grimly. 'People just put up with her.'

'My father didn't. Oh, he did for twenty years or so, but then he wised up.' He gave her an apologetic smile. 'She means well.'

It was too much. Daphne lost her temper. 'Means well?' she cried. 'You've no idea what I've been putting up with all day. Sly innuendo ... I don't care if she *is* your mother.' Her voice dropped, but it was no less intense. 'Des, I'm not putting up with much more of this. So don't be surprised if you come home from work one day and find ...'

'Find what?'

'Oh, I'll think of something.' She would – she was damned sure she would.

But things didn't get any better; instead they got worse. The next thing Daphne learnt was that Mrs Clarke had taken to inviting Julie Robinson from next door into the house when she wasn't there – and it was perfectly clear what her intention was – she had taken it on herself to do a spot of matchmaking. Daphne told him that his mother was making a fuss over Julie, and Des had been surprised that his mother had even known Julie. But it seemed that they had met in the front yard the other morning while Julie was on her way to work. Mrs Clarke reproached Des for not having mentioned Julie in his letters to her, to which he had retorted that he didn't have to put *everything* in his letters. Julie, as it turned out, had told his mother about Lorraine and the collapse of the wedding plans, and Julie had hoped Des didn't mind her telling his mother this, but she knew how much it would hurt him to talk about it and, well, his mother really ought to know what had happened.

Des knew what his mother was trying to do. He told her she was wasting her time. He definitely wasn't interested in Julie, even if, as his mother claimed, Julie was still carrying a torch for him. If she wanted to invite Julie to the house, she was welcome to go ahead, but she shouldn't expect him to be there. 'Oh no, dear,' Mrs Clarke had protested. 'I won't interfere with you, or Julie, or any other girl for that matter.'

When Des had asked her if she was referring to Daphne, she had said, not Daphne, but all the girls who may cross his path in the years to come. And what did she mean by that? Years to come? She wouldn't be here in years to come. Oh, but she would, she lovingly assured him, because she had arranged for an estate agent in Perth to rent her house, and she would be staying with him for a long, long time ... and was anything the matter with him? He looked quite ill.

When he told her that his mother intended to stay on in the house, Daphne was appalled – but it *was* Des's house, and there was nothing she could do about it. *She* would be the one who would have to move out if she didn't like it.

When Mrs Clarke asked her if Des had told her what she had decided, Daphne put the best face she could on it. There was no point in letting the woman see that she was upset. 'Yes, he did as a matter of fact,' she said with equanimity.

'Oh.' Mrs Clarke looked a little disconcerted. Probably she had expected Daphne to pack her things and move out the moment she heard the news. 'I hope that doesn't put you out.'

'Of course it doesn't,' Daphne breezily assured her. She wasn't going to give her any sort of satisfaction.

She and Des were on their way out. She was working tonight at one of the local clubs, and Des had said he would come along with her, to see for himself, as he had told her, just exactly what she did in her act. Daphne didn't mind. Perhaps it would put his mind at rest.

Mrs Clarke had seemed a little displeased by the fact that they were going out. *She* hadn't been told about it. Now she asked them where they were going.

'Didn't Des tell you?' Daphne was going to enjoy this. 'He's coming to watch me work.'

'Work?' Mrs Clarke was shocked. 'Taking your clothes off...'

'That's right,' Daphne said cheerfully. 'I would have asked you as well, but I'm afraid it's for men only.'

Mrs Clarke had shrunk back in her chair. Her hand fluttered weakly. 'Desmond... my tablets.'

Daphne and Des had been expecting something like this to happen, and had discussed what they would do when it did. So, as she gasped, and her hand fluttered, and her face twisted in pain, Daphne fetched her a glass of water while Des found her bottle of pills.

'Oh ... oh ... don't leave me ... Desmond.'

'Don't worry, Mum, you'll be in perfectly good hands.' Crossing to the telephone, Des picked up the receiver and began to dial.

'Desmond ... ?'

But Desmond was already speaking to the doctor. 'Sorry to bother you on a Saturday night,' he was saying after having introduced himself, 'but it's my mother. She's having a heart attack.' He covered the mouthpiece with his hand and turned to his mother who was watching him fearfully. 'That's what you're having, isn't it, Mum?' When his mother, still moaning, managed a shaky nod, he uncovered the mouthpiece and said, quite calmly, 'Yeah, it's got all the elements of a heart attack. Yeah ... well, you know the address. I'll see you shortly.' He hung up. 'Well, he's on his way.' He said to Daphne, 'You may as well go ahead. I'll catch up with you after the doctor's been.'

'No ...' Mrs Clarke was moaning again. 'Don't leave me ... Desmond.'

Des was cool. 'Don't worry, Mum. If there are any problems, Doctor Murray will run you straight to hospital.'

'Hospital?' Mrs Clarke looked startled.

'Yes, and you can thank Daphne for that. She

made all the arrangements.'

Daphne smiled at Mrs Clarke with great solicitude. 'If we're all going to be living together, Mrs Clarke, we'll naturally want to take good care of you.' She backed towards the door. 'Goodnight – and good luck.'

As Des told her later – and as they both suspected – the doctor, after he had examined Mrs Clarke, was unable to find any evidence of a heart problem. In fact, for a woman of her age, she was in perfect shape. Her blood pressure was normal, her lungs were clear, her reflexes were good – and Mrs Clarke protested that there were some things that couldn't be expected to show in such a cursory examination. The doctor agreed, and said he wanted to see her in his surgery first thing on Monday morning.

It was shortly after this that the poison pen letters began to appear.

Most of the people in the street received one of these letters, directed against Daphne, her profession, her morals, and urging the recipients to band together to force her out of the street. They were anonymous, as were the telephone calls Daphne herself received.

It was Helen Daniels next door who told Daphne about the letter that had been slipped under the Robinson's door. 'You must realise it's just some crank,' she said. 'Most of the people in the street don't care what you do.'

When Daphne asked to see the letter, Helen told her that Paul Robinson had it, but she could tell Daphne that it was fairly disgusting.

The medical tests on Mrs Clarke proved there was nothing whatsoever wrong with her. Des brought the results home, and told his mother she would be pleased to learn that she wouldn't need to take any more of those pills of hers. He picked up the bottle, and against her protests told her that the whole lot could now go down the toilet. Mrs Clarke was thunderstruck.

The following morning, Daphne found a note under the front door. She scanned it briefly, then angrily crumpled it in her hand and threw it into the rubbish bin.

'It's no use throwing them away,' Mrs Clarke observed quietly behind her. 'They'll just keep coming.'

Daphne was very angry. 'Who *writes* that filth?' she demanded.

'Respectable people who care about the neighbourhood.'

Daphne could hardly contain herself. This woman was so . . . so damned *smug*. 'Is that *your* idea of respectable?'

Mrs Clarke stood there with her arms folded, her expression grim. 'Why don't you just pack up and leave?' she suggested coldly. 'Don't you think you've done enough harm?'

'Harm?' Daphne forced herself to remain

calm. 'What harm?'

'My son's reputation for a start. Can't you see that people don't want your sort around here?'

'And what precisely *is* my sort, Mrs Clarke?' With difficulty, Daphne managed to keep her voice level.

'The sort that takes her clothes off for men ... for money, and for goodness knows what else.'

It was too much for Daphne to stand. 'It's lucky I respect your age, if nothing else, Mrs Clarke,' she cried. 'Otherwise I'd belt you right across that ... that smug face of yours.'

'That's only to be expected.' There was cold, implacable hatred in the older woman's eyes. 'That's the talk of the gutter, and it seems to me that's where you belong. So why don't you go back there and stop hurting a decent, respectable boy like my son?'

'You're obsessed with that word respectable, aren't you?' Daphne shouted bitterly.

Mrs Clarke faced her squarely. 'If you had any decency whatsoever, a prospect I find highly unlikely, you would pack up and move away from here. You've upset too many people.'

'Oh-ho, upset them, have I?' Daphne's cheeks were burning. Her finger violently jabbed the air between them. 'And what about the twisted mind who's behind this campaign against me?'

'It's not easy to stir people into action,' Mrs Clarke remarked.

'You seem to know a lot about it,' Daphne said suspiciously.

'Why don't you take my advice – and move.'

'And give you the satisfaction?' Daphne stormed to the front door. 'No fear.'

Of the neighbours, the one with whom Mrs Clarke seemed to be on the best terms was Mrs Brown across the street, and they did have one thing in common – they both wanted to see the last of Daphne. Mrs Brown was just the sort of woman to lend a sympathetic ear to Mrs Clarke's complaints. She would have agreed with Mrs Clarke that it was a disgrace that a mother should have moved all the way from Perth, away from her friends and everyone she knew, to be with her son, only to find he was living with the sort of woman for whom it was only a matter of time before she started bringing men home to Ramsay Street. Mrs Brown would have agreed with her that a girl like Daphne didn't belong in Ramsay Street.

When her engagement at the Ferndale Angling Club was cancelled as the result of a bomb hoax, Daphne decided she had had enough. When she returned to the house that night, and Des asked her why she was back so early, she told him in disgust what had happened. 'I mean, have you ever heard of anything so ludicrous?' she exclaimed, flinging her bag down on the couch.

'A practical joke,' Des observed.

Mrs Clarke was there. The television was on. 'Oh, of course it turned out to be a hoax,' Daphne said shortly, 'but the police were called and the place had to be evacuated. The evening was called off after that.' And that meant she hadn't been paid, which made it worse.

'How unfortunate.' Mrs Clarke had a self-satisfied smirk on her lips.

'Have they got any idea who was responsible?' Des asked.

'No. Just that it was a woman.'

Mrs Clarke stood up. 'Well, if you'll excuse me,' she said to Des, pointedly ignoring Daphne, 'I'm a little tired, so I think I'll turn in. Goodnight, Desmond.' She left the room without even looking at Daphne.

Daphne perched herself on the arm of the couch. She felt tired, completely done in. 'I'm sorry, Des,' she said wearily, 'but I can't take much more. Your mother is a pain, and I've had her right up to here. I don't know if she's behind the "get Daphne" campaign and I couldn't care less now. I'm moving out of here.'

Des began to protest, but she silenced him with a wave of her hand. What she really needed now was a good stiff drink. 'I'll look for a place first thing in the morning,' she told him, pushing herself up from the arm of the couch and heading for her bedroom.

Des was quick to act. He told Daphne later

what he had done. 'My mother's moving out,' he said.

Daphne had been looking at flats all day, but hadn't really found one that suited her. She was tired and her feet were sore. 'Really?'

'She's in her room now. Packing. I've rented a flat for her.'

'You did what?' This was good news to Daphne. 'Can you afford it?'

'Well, I'll be up to my eyeballs in debt, but it's worth it.'

He told her how he had given his mother no choice. He had come home earlier and told her that he was going to show her her new home. She had been puzzled. She was already in her new home, she had said. Then he had told her about the flat he had rented for her. She would love it, he had said. Of course she had protested, tried to find all sorts of excuses but, showing the determination he realised he should have displayed at the outset, he overruled every one of her objections. It was all arranged. She had to go.

Daphne was delighted to hear the news. 'And there's more.' Des sounded quite pleased with himself. 'I've found out who is behind that campaign against you. Of course Mum knew about it. I forced it out of her. She said she had promised Carol Brown she wouldn't say anything about it, when I pressed her, and of course that gave the game away. I've had a word with her, too, laid it on the line. I gave her one hell of a fright.' He smiled broadly. 'She won't do it again,' he said.

Daphne looked around the room, and breathed a huge sigh of relief. It was good to have the place to themselves again.

6

The bad blood between Danny Ramsay and
Carol Brown really stemmed from the time
Danny stopped one of her kids from running out
onto the road after a ball. Seeing little Josie about
to run out onto the road, he scooped her up in his
arms, just as Mrs Brown came charging towards
him from her front gate.

'Get your hands off my child,' she cried
furiously.

Danny lowered Josie to the footpath. Josie ran
to her mother. Danny was stunned. 'I never did
anything,' he protested.

But Mrs Brown was screaming at him. She was
waving her arms around. She had probably been
drinking again; everyone knew she drank a lot.
'Go on, go on. Go and bully someone your own
size, Danny Ramsay. Your father will be hearing
about this.'

Danny was stung by the injustice of it. He had
just stopped Josie from running out onto the

road, and if he hadn't, and if a car had been coming . . . 'Don't pick on me,' he shouted back at her. 'She was going to run out onto the road.'

But Mrs Brown wasn't listening to him. She was quite livid with rage. 'Get out before I call the police,' she screamed.

'Go on, call the police,' Danny yelled back at her. 'Go on, do it, and see what happens to people who tell lies.'

And of course Max had blown up at him when Mrs Brown told her side of the story, and he refused to listen to what Danny had to say about it. His mother urged him to apologise to Mrs Brown, but he said there was no way he would apologise to her. It was Mrs Brown who owed *him* an apology.

When, a couple of weeks later, he and Scott Robinson were down near the shopping centre, and he saw Mrs Brown walking ahead of them, very carefully, he noticed, in the manner of someone who had been drinking and didn't want to show it, his resentment surfaced again.

Reaching a side street, Mrs Brown turned the corner. Danny walked on, while Scott lingered behind to study the window display of a store that sold sound equipment. Before he reached the corner, Danny noticed a guy running out of the side street and turning in the opposite direction.

When he came to the street, he glanced along it, and was startled to see Mrs Brown lying on the footpath. Assuming that she had lost her balance and fallen, Danny hurried up to her. Her handbag was lying open by her side. He bent over her. 'What happened?'

Then she began to scream. 'Help! Police! I've been robbed.' Danny backed away. She was staring straight up at him. 'Someone help me! Stop him!'

Danny panicked. Scott was just turning into the street. Danny ran up to him. 'Get out of here,' he shouted. Mrs Brown was still screaming.

And now people were beginning to appear. Someone shouted, 'Hey! Stop those boys!'

Danny and Scott kept running until they had reached the park. Danny slowed down, then stopped and waited for Scott to catch up with him. They were both out of breath. Scott sank down against a tree. 'What did you do?'

'Nothing,' Danny panted.

'Then what are we running away for?'

Danny dropped down beside him. For the moment they were safe. 'I came round the corner and Mrs Brown was lying there in a heap. I was going to help her, but then she started screaming blue murder.'

Scott still didn't understand. 'If you didn't *do* anything, why are we running?'

'Because I freaked out,' Danny replied sharply. 'Okay?'

'Terrific,' Scott groaned.

Danny knew now it had been the wrong thing to do, but he hadn't been thinking clearly; it had all happened so suddenly. 'Yeah, I know.'

'You know how this is going to look, don't you?'

Danny looked at him. 'Well, why did *you* run?'

'Because I'm your mate,' Scott replied simply.

What a mess. Danny tried to think. It would soon be dark, and maybe the police were already at the house, asking for him.

'Are you sure she recognised you?' Scott asked.

'I don't know.'

'Why don't we just go back and explain what happened?'

'Oh, yeah, sure . . .'

'Tell the truth. What else can we do?'

'My word against hers.' Danny snorted derisively. 'No problem.'

'*Somebody* must have seen what happened.'

No such luck. 'The street was empty.'

'Are you sure of that?'

The shadows were lengthening, and there was already a chill in the air. 'No. I'm not sure of anything,' Danny said miserably. 'All I know is, I've been set up.'

Scott was still trying to look on the bright side. 'Maybe we're not in trouble at all. Maybe Mrs Brown has already realised she's in the wrong. Maybe we've got nothing to worry about.'

'Maybe, maybe.' Danny was frightened. He

was on edge. 'Use your brains, why don't you? That woman hates my guts. Look how she got me into trouble, said I was bullying her kid. Even if she *did* realise she was wrong, she wouldn't say so.'

'I still say somebody must have seen what happened,' Scott murmured.

Danny had an idea. He looked at Scott shrewdly. 'Suppose *you* did.'

'But I didn't.'

'But suppose you *said* you did.'

'I can't do that.'

'Look, Scotty.' Danny scrambled round onto his knees to face his companion. 'It would work. Think about it. You came around the corner, and you saw the whole thing.'

'No, no.' Scott was beginning to sound agitated. 'You're only making things worse.'

'Then you think *I* did it, don't you?' Danny said bitterly.

'Of course I don't.'

'Well?' Ah, what was the use? Danny slumped back against the tree. 'Forget it,' he muttered.

Then Scott changed his mind. 'All right then,' he said. 'I'll do it.'

That was better. Danny sprang to his feet. 'Come on, let's go.'

It was almost dark by the time they reached Ramsay Street. Danny's heart sank when he saw the police car outside the Robinsons' house. Both boys were frightened, and Danny tried to cheer Scott up by saying they might as well face up to it, they would have some time, and they had nothing to lose. They moved silently around to the back of the house and, opening the back door, stepped into the kitchen. They hesitated when they heard voices in the other room. Max Ramsay was saying aggressively, 'Now listen, Sergeant, I think you're taking a fair bit for granted. I mean, this Mrs Brown is a bit of a trouble maker in the street, you know, and she's had it in for Danny for some time.'

Then there was another, unfamiliar voice. 'We're not relying entirely on her statement, Mr Ramsay. Three people saw them running away from the scene. One of them, the manager of one of the stores, says he knows both boys.'

'But Danny wouldn't do anything like that,' Max protested.

'And Scott's never been in trouble before,' Helen Daniels added. 'It's impossible.'

In the kitchen, Danny looked at Scott and nodded. Scott nodded back at him. Danny took a deep breath. It was time to make an appearance. They moved to the living room doorway. Max saw them first.

'Where the hell have you been?' he demanded in a raised voice.

'Out,' Danny replied.

Max bore down on him angrily. 'I want a

straight answer from you.'

They were all staring at the two boys – Max, Scott's father and grandmother, the police sergeant and the woman constable who held an open notebook in her hand. The sergeant took a step closer to them. 'Were either of you two boys near the shopping centre this afternoon?'

'Yes,' Danny answered.

'I see.' The sergeant nodded. 'Well now, I'll have to ask you both to come down to the station with your parents.' He looked at Max, then at Jim Robinson. 'You'll both need to be present while we question the boys.'

'Now hang on,' Max protested. 'Can't we sort this thing out here?'

'This is not a juvenile misdemeanour, Mr Ramsay,' the sergeant said grimly with a shake of his head. 'This is robbery with assault. It's a very serious matter.'

At the police station, the boys were interviewed separately. Danny told his story, but he knew the sergeant didn't believe him. He was very frightened. Their statements were typed up and signed, and they were released under cognisance of their parents until such time as the case came before a magistrate.

When they returned to the house, Max told a worried Maria what had happened. He said he would try and get Mrs Brown to change her story because she had to be mistaken. Scott, he said, had backed up Danny's version of the story, so they were on good solid ground there.

But Mrs Brown turned out to be adamant when Max went to see her. She had made no mistake. She virtually ordered Max out of her house.

Even so, it was her word against Danny's, and there was a good chance of them getting off, Max told Jim Robinson, when the matter came before the court. And that might have been so if Scott hadn't inadvertently let slip the fact to his father the morning after a sleepless night that he had kept dreaming about what had happened; it was like an old movie, him walking around the corner and seeing Danny crouched beside Mrs Brown... Jim Robinson picked this up immediately. It wasn't what Scott had told the police. What he had told the police was that when he had turned the corner he had seen Mrs Brown lying on the ground and Danny walking towards her. It was a significant difference. Jim Robinson said he would have to inform the police. Max was furious. Danny was dismayed when he heard about it. It seemed there was no chance for him at all now that Scott had been caught out in a lie.

Scott was abject when Danny tapped on his bedroom window that night, then climbing into the room, sarcastically thanked him for dumping him the way he had.

'It was a mistake,' Scott told him miserably,

'and Dad picked it up.' He grimaced painfully. 'So I'm a lousy liar.'

Danny was a little mollified. The damage had been done, and there was nothing they could do about it now. 'We're gone for sure now, aren't we?'

'Yeah, I guess so,' Danny sighed. Things didn't look too good at all. 'The worst you're going to get is a twelve month good behaviour bond. But I reckon there's a good chance that I'll be locked up.'

His father had thought so, too. He had seen a solicitor who, he said, had pulled no punches. He had told Max that the magistrate might go easy on them both if the money and purse belonging to Mrs Brown were returned and they pleaded guilty. When Danny had protested for the umpteenth time that he hadn't done it, Max had glumly resigned himself to the fact that the case was lost.

'There's no way I'm going to plead guilty,' Danny told Scott. 'I'm telling the truth, whatever happens. But I reckon *you're* off the hook.'

They were sitting on the edge of Scott's bed. Scott looked at him. 'How come?'

'When you changed your statement to the police . . . that means you never actually saw what happened. You couldn't have had anything to do with Mrs Brown being robbed – and I'll back you up.'

'Thanks, Danny. I really appreciate that.'

'Well, you did try to back *me* up, even if you did louse it up.'

'They'll probably think we're just telling more lies,' Scott said unhappily. 'Let's face it, if our own fathers won't believe us, why should the magistrate?'

Danny made up his mind to do something he had been toying with all day. 'You know what?'

'What?'

'I'm clearing out of here.'

'Where?'

'I haven't worked that out yet. Just somewhere.'

Scott stood up. 'Then I'm coming with you,' he said resolutely.

Later that night, after everyone was asleep, the two boys wheeled their bikes silently out of their respective yards. Each of them had a hastily packed knapsack on his back. They met in the park as they had arranged, then together pedalled northwards into the mild moonlit night.

They were still pedalling when the sky began to lighten. The city was miles behind them. Fields stretched away from both sides of the road. The boys were tired, but they still kept pedalling. They were cycling down a hill when one of Danny's tyres burst, the bike swerved and Danny was thrown onto the embankment.

He wasn't hurt, but there was no way he could

fix the tyre, which, he saw, had been punctured by a jagged piece of glass on the road. Neither he nor Scott had a patch in their kit large enough to cover the hole. Fortunately, the bike itself wasn't damaged.

They decided to try and hitch a lift into the nearest town where they could get the tyre fixed. When Danny expressed reservations about anyone stopping to pick them up, Scott thought that maybe a pick-up truck would come along.

As it was, with the sun becoming hotter and the nearest town more than 20 kilometres away, it wasn't a pick-up truck that finally stopped for them, but a panel van. There were surfboards attached to the top of the van. The driver and his mate were both young, no more than a year or two older than Scott and Danny. At the driver's suggestion, Scott and Danny secured their bikes and knapsacks to the roof.

As they were driving towards the town, the driver asked them how long they had been on the road. Danny grinned and told them, then went on, 'We told the folks to stick it, so ... here we are.'

'Yeah?' The driver's eyes caught Danny's in the rear vision mirror. 'And how are they going to handle that?'

'Well, we didn't actually tell them. We thought that when they found us gone, they'd work it out for themselves.'

'So no one knows where you are, huh?'

Scott nudged Danny. 'Nope,' Danny said. 'That's the way we like it.'

They were dropped off at the town's only garage. Thanking the two guys, Scott and Danny clambered out of the back of the van and prepared to loosen the straps that held their bikes and knapsacks in place on the roof. But before they could do this, the engine was suddenly revved, and the van roared along the dusty street as Scott and Danny stared after it in total dismay.

They were stranded. All they had between them was fifteen dollars and a few cents. They would have had more, but Scott's money had been in his knapsack.

Disconsolately, they walked past the petrol pumps to the service station. In the window were a number of cards, announcements of one sort or another, articles for sale, and one, Danny noticed, offering work for casual labourers. He pointed it out to Scott.

'What do you reckon?' Scott asked.

'It's better than starving,' Danny replied.

The farm looked run down. Standing by the gate, taking in the neglected condition of the house and the paddocks, Scott and Danny began to have second thoughts. But as Scott reminded Danny, they didn't have much choice. The money they had wouldn't carry them far, and when Danny suggested that they could always sell Scott's watch, Scott wondered who would buy it, and for how much, and anyway it had his name and telephone number engraved on the back, which would be a giveaway. Danny had to reluctantly agree. As Scott had said, they didn't have much choice.

It had been a long walk from the town. They were both tired, hot and dusty. They hadn't known what to expect. The guy at the garage had told them that the Forbeses were the most miserable old codgers they could ever hope to meet. Real battleaxes they were, he had said – and the boys were full of trepidation as to how they would be received when they reached the farm. There was no other work for them in the town, the guy at the garage had informed them.

They were still hesitating beside the gate when they heard a shout. 'Hoy, you there.' An old woman was coming towards them from the house. She looked quite fierce. 'What are you doing there?'

'We've come about the job,' Scott told her.

'Oh yes?' She regarded them suspiciously. Her face was leathery and deeply lined, her hair grey and stringy. 'What are your names then?'

'I'm Danny.' Danny pointed to Scott. 'He's Scott. 'Ah . . .' He looked at Scott for inspiration. 'Jones. Danny and Scott Jones. We . . . we're brothers.'

Mrs Forbes was obviously unimpressed as she

looked them over very carefully. 'You look a bit scrawny to me,' she pronounced at last. 'Have you done this sort of work before?'

'We practically grew up on a farm,' Scott said glibly.

Mrs Forbes subjected them to another long and critical scrutiny, then exhaled noisily. 'Well, I don't suppose I got much choice,' she grunted.

'Does that mean we've got the job?' Danny asked eagerly.

'I don't know what I'm doing, hiring a couple of namby pambies like you,' the old woman said in disgust, 'but, yes, I suppose you'll have to do for the want of anyone better.' She turned away and began to head towards the barn next to the house. After she had gone a short distance, she stopped and glared back at them. 'Well, get a move on,' she commanded. 'I haven't got all day.'

The boys grinned at each other, then began to hurry after her. 'And shut the gate,' she called back to them.

She led them into the barn, which was just as ramshackle as the house. She pointed to a couple of straw pallets on the floor of the barn. 'This is where you sleep,' she told them gruffly. 'I'm not having strangers in the house.' She took down some folded blankets from a shelf near the door and thrust them into Danny's arms. Then she jerked her head towards the door. 'There's a tap outside where you can wash up. It's bore water –

so if you want fresh water, you'll have to come and see me about it.'

But there was something more important that Danny needed to know. 'How much do we get paid?' he asked.

Mrs Forbes gave him a stony look. 'Oh, I was wondering when you would bring that up. It's forty dollars a day each. There's only a couple of days' work in it, but you won't see a penny of it until the job's finished, and finished properly.'

'What sort of work is it?' Scott queried.

'Digging.'

'Digging what?'

'Digging a manure pit.'

They were put straight to work. Mrs Forbes showed them where the pit was to be dug, told them where to find the pick and shovel, and left them to it. They began to dig.

The ground was hard, and the sun was hot. They took off their shirts and draped them over the fence. Scott took off his watch and placed it on the fence post next to the shirts.

It seemed they were making hardly any impression on the stony soil. Sweat streamed down their bodies. 'Forty dollars for this,' Danny complained. 'Who needs it?'

'We do,' Scott muttered – and Danny couldn't deny the truth of it. He kept digging.

After about an hour, they heard a car start up, then a few moments later, Mrs Forbes pulled up alongside the fence in a very old car. 'If that's an hour's work,' she called caustically across to them, 'then I'd hate to see what you call a day's work.'

'What do you mean?' Danny was stung. 'We haven't stopped.'

'Stop wasting time,' Mrs Forbes snapped. 'I'm going out for a while now, and while I'm gone I don't want you two slacking off.'

'Don't worry,' Scott assured her. 'We won't.'

'How long are you going to be?' Danny wanted to know.

'Long as it takes,' the old woman replied brusquely, giving them both a steely look before putting the car into gear and driving off down the road in a cloud of dust.

'Old cow,' Danny snorted, leaning on his shovel. 'She's probably off to the pub.'

'Yeah.' Scott wiped the sweat from his forehead with the back of his hand. 'And that's probably why her husband left her – she's an alkie.'

'You reckon he left her?'

'Well, he's not here, is he?'

'She probably bumped him off,' Danny remarked.

'Yeah, and she's hidden the body until we've finished digging the grave.'

They looked at each other. Was it possible? No, it was too ludicrous. They laughed.

They were making slow progress. Neither of them were used to such heavy toil. After about two hours they heard the car coming back up the road. Once again, the car stopped by the fence. Mrs Forbes climbed out and crossed to the fence. She pointed to one end of the hole the boys had dug. 'It needs to be a bit longer . . . that way.'

To Danny, she seemed to be a little different, more subdued somehow than she had been before she had left. 'We haven't had time for that part yet,' he told her.

'Just making sure,' she said.

'We've done all right, haven't we?' Scott asked her.

'Oh, I've seen worse,' she remarked off-handedly. She noticed Scott's watch which had fallen from the fence post onto the ground, and bent to pick it up. She replaced it on the post.

That night, they planned to go down to the pub after they had cleaned themselves up and eaten, thinking that they might pass for nineteen or twenty – or eighteen, anyway – but no sooner had they ravenously attacked the corned beef, boiled cabbage and mashed potatoes Mrs Forbes had brought out to them in the barn, than they fell into a deep, exhausted sleep. It had been a long and tiring day.

Danny woke up, startled; something had hit him on the chest. He looked blankly up at the old woman standing beside him, and for a moment he didn't recognise her nor did he know where he was. 'Come on,' she said briskly. 'I've brought your breakfast.'

Scott sat up and yawned loudly. 'What time is it?'

It was still dark outside. 'Just after six,' Mrs Forbes replied.

'You're kidding,' Danny groaned. 'It's still night time.'

Mrs Forbes' eyes narrowed suspiciously. 'I thought you would be used to country hours, being brought up on a farm and all that.'

Scott and Danny exchanged a quick, worried glance. 'Ah... we've been in the city for a few months,' Scott said quickly. 'We're a bit out of touch.'

'Well, you'd better get *in* touch again, quick smart.' She pointed to the tray she had set on the bench against the wall. 'There's your breakfast. I want you out and working by seven.'

'Seven?' Danny wailed.

Mrs Forbes moved to the door. 'If you've got a union, complain to it. I've got hens to feed.'

About halfway through the morning, Scott and Danny, already hot and dirty, went into the kitchen of the house for a drink of water. Mrs Forbes sat at the kitchen table, shelling peas.

'I don't know,' she said disapprovingly as Scott refilled his glass at the sink. 'You'll never get the job done if you keep stopping like that. It's a good thing I'm here to keep an eye on you.'

'You don't have to keep an eye on us, Mrs Forbes,' Danny said defensively. 'We're not going to run off, or anything.'

'No. You can't afford to, can you?' For some reason, Mrs Forbes found this amusing. 'Tell you what, though,' she continued. 'I'll leave you to it if you tell me one thing.' She looked at them both closely. 'What are you running from?'

'Nothing.' Danny was alarmed. 'We're not running from anything.'

Mrs Forbes looked up at the ceiling. 'That's funny. I don't see any pigs flying up there.'

'What?'

She fixed them both with a stony gaze. 'Because you're running away from something. I don't care what it is, but if you're running from the police, you can get out right now.'

What did she know? Danny's alarm was mounting. 'We haven't done anything – honestly.'

'Doesn't answer my question, does it?' Mrs Forbes said grimly.

Danny was thinking hard. 'All right,' he said. 'We are running away.'

'Danny...' Scott was frowning at him.

'But we haven't done anything wrong. You see, our Dad, he used to bash us when he got drunk.'

Mrs Forbes nodded wisely. 'There's nothing new about that. A lot of men get like that when they're on the booze.'

'Yeah, but . . .' Danny was improvising wildly; he was rather impressed with himself. 'He was mean. Meaner than anybody. About six months ago, he hit Scott so hard that he almost broke his arm.'

Now Scott was joining in. 'He would have killed me next time . . . if we had stayed.'

Mrs Forbes was looking at them doubtfully. 'We took some food and stuff,' Danny told her, warming to his story. 'Nothing important. Later on we found out he had reported us to the cops.'

'We don't know that for a fact,' Scott supplied, 'but it's not worth going back to find out.' He paused for effect. 'That's the truth, Mrs Forbes.'

'Sounds like a yarn to me,' she said dubiously.

'It's not,' Danny said fervently. 'We could tell you things about our old man that would make your hair stand on end.'

'I doubt it.'

'You're not going to turn us in, are you?' Danny asked anxiously.

'I might,' she replied slowly, 'but then again I might not. The most important thing to me right now is to get that pit dug before the rain starts. And if you keep yakking the way you are, then it will never get done.'

During the afternoon, she came out to see how they were progressing with the pit. It was true that they weren't making much progress, but they were doing their best. She began to ask them questions, and to Danny it seemed as if she were putting them to some sort of test. For instance, there were questions about their fictitious father. How was she to know, she asked, that they were telling the truth about him? For all she knew, he might be quite a nice sort of bloke.

But Danny had an answer for that one. 'Oh, he fools some people,' he said. 'He comes across as quite reasonable then.'

Mrs Forbes was still curious about this so-called father of theirs. 'Would they say he would be the kind of fellow who would trick someone into coming home by pretending everything was hunky-dory?'

'You've got it in one,' Scott said.

Danny was puzzled by the questions. 'You do believe us, don't you?'

'I don't know,' Mrs Forbes replied thoughtfully. 'I might do, but then again I might not.'

There was something funny going on, Scott and Danny decided after the old woman had returned to the house. They didn't like the way she had been questioning them, and decided the best thing they could do was finish the job, collect their money and get out of there as soon as they possibly could because there was no telling what a loony, as they were convinced she was, might do next.

When they had finished digging the pit, Mrs

Forbes examined it critically, then pronounced that she supposed it would have to do. But when Danny suggested they might now be paid, she told them that the job was only half-completed. The pit had to be filled in yet, and they would find the bags of manure in the shed behind the house. Once that was done, they would be paid. The boys protested. All she had told them to do was dig the pit; she had told them nothing about filling it with manure. But they had no choice, she told them, if they wanted to be paid. Grudgingly, they set to work.

When they had finally filled the pit, they cleaned themselves up as best they could from the tap outside the house, then set out to collect their wages. As they were coming around the side of the house, they froze. A police car was heading up the rutted driveway. Danny yanked Scott back out of sight. 'She's split on us,' he muttered angrily. 'The old cow's gone and split on us.'

'Maybe they're coming for something else,' Scott suggested.

'Like what? I'm sure not sticking around to find out.'

'We can't go yet. We haven't got the money.'

'What use is it going to be in gaol?' Danny demanded.

But Scott stood firm. 'I don't care. I'm not leaving without it. You can go if you're scared.'

Danny was scared – bloody scared – but he

wasn't about to show it. 'Who's scared?' he said defiantly.

Moving around the back of the house to the shed, they could see the uniformed policeman talking to Mrs Forbes on the verandah. They were too far away to hear what was being said, except that both of them were looking very serious, and it was quite clear that this wasn't just a social call. After a few minutes, the policeman returned to his car, and Mrs Forbes disappeared back inside the house.

They waited until the car had gone, then quickly crossed back to the house and knocked on the kitchen door. There was no response. Scott knocked again, more loudly. 'Mrs Forbes!' he called.

'Go away.' The muffled voice came from inside.

'We've finished the job, Mrs Forbes.'

When there was no further reply, Scott opened the door and the boys stepped hesitantly into the kitchen. Mrs Forbes was sitting at the table, her hands clasped together, with an expression of shock on her face.

'Are you all right?' Danny asked in concern.

She looked up at them. 'Of course I'm all right,' she snapped. 'Why shouldn't I be all right?'

But it was quite obvious that she wasn't. All the colour had drained from her face; she looked terrible. You're not sick, or anything?'

There was some money on the table in front of her. She nodded to it. 'There's your money,' she said distantly. 'Just take it, and go.'

Moving across to the table, Danny picked up the money. He looked uncertainly at the old woman, but she seemed no longer to be aware of their presence in the room.

They had reached the gate, and were turning along the road towards town when a truck pulled up alongside them. An old man with grey stubble on his jaw climbed out and faced them. 'How's the old woman?' he asked. 'The local copper just told me her husband died in hospital.'

Danny and Scott exchanged startled glances. That explained everything. 'Her husband?'

The old man nodded. 'Well, whether he was her husband or not doesn't matter much now, does it? Anyway, for what it's worth, I'm sorry for her. It must have been tough running the farm on her own, what with going to the hospital to see him every day for months.'

Danny, too, was feeling sorry for the old woman. She had told them nothing about her husband being in hospital – and they had joked about her heading to the pub when they had seen her driving off in that old car of hers. 'What was wrong with him?'

'Don't ask me.' The old farmer climbed back into his truck. 'They kept to themselves. Nobody around here had much to do with them.'

After he had driven off, Scott and Danny remained by the gate, undecided. They couldn't leave her now, they thought, alone in her grief. If there was only something they could say to her, some small comfort they could provide ... They returned to the house.

Mrs Forbes was still sitting at the kitchen table. Spread out in front of her was an old pocket watch, a pair of spectacles, a penknife, and a badly scuffed leather wallet. She was gazing at an old photograph with tears in her eyes. When she saw Scott and Danny, she put the photograph down, and quickly brushed her hand across her eyes.

'Oh, come for your money, have you?'

'No, you've already paid us, Mrs Forbes.'

'Well, you'd better finish digging that pit then.'

'We have.'

'Oh ... yes, all right. Well, you'd better be on your way then.'

She was still in shock. Her mind was wandering. 'We've just heard about your husband,' Scott told her.

She looked at them bleakly. 'Would you like a cup of tea, Mrs Forbes?' Danny asked her.

'Yes,' she replied after a brief pause. 'Thank you, Danny. A cup of tea would be very nice.'

While they were waiting for the kettle to boil, she showed them the photograph in which a much younger Mrs Forbes and a fair haired man were laughing happily at the camera. 'Oh, we laughed,' she said with a sad, reflective smile. 'We laughed all the time. That was the joke, you see. All the busybodies in the town... they thought we were old sauerkraut and bully. They didn't even think we were married when we first moved here – but we were. We were married, and we were happy. When the stickbeaks came around we'd bung on the bad tempered act and yell abuse at each other.' She sighed. 'Then, when it was all over... Ned would put his arms around me... and we would laugh.'

Danny was feeling a little uncomfortable; he had never been faced with this sort of situation before. 'Mrs Forbes, do you have any relatives?' he asked.

'No.' There was some pride in her voice as she said it. 'No one. Ned used to say we were Darby and Joan against the world. That's who we were – Darby and Joan...' There was a break in her voice, and her eyes filled with tears. She shook her head briskly. 'Don't take any notice of me. I'm just being silly. Now you two had better get going. It will soon be dark.'

There was something more Danny wanted to ask her. He and Scott had discussed it on their way back to the house. 'Ah... we were wondering, Mrs Forbes. Could we have the job back... for a while longer?'

It was agreed. Mrs Forbes told them they could stay as long as they liked; there was still a lot of work to be done around the place, and she would also welcome the company. But first, arrangements had to be made for the funeral. It would be very simple; she didn't have the money for a lavish affair– and, anyway, Ned wouldn't have wanted anything fancy.

Danny first noticed there was something wrong when he encountered Mrs Forbes on her knees, vigorously scrubbing the kitchen floor. When he told her that he and Scott were on their way down to fix the fence, she glared furiously up at him.

'Who the hell told you to walk all over my clean floor?' she demanded.

Danny was taken aback. 'Eh?'

'I've just finished scrubbing that floor.' Her eyes narrowed suspiciously. 'What are you doing here, anyway?'

Perturbed by her attitude, Danny stepped back from the still wet section of the floor. 'Are you okay, Mrs Forbes?'

'You young hooligans, tormenting people,'the old woman cried. 'You think it's funny, don't you, to throw stones on our roof?' She straightened, and pointed to the corner where she kept her shot-gun. 'You see that shot-gun over there? You ever come back here again, and I'll use it on you.'

'Mrs Forbes, I'm Danny,' he said anxiously.

'Danny?' She frowned, and peered at him more closely. Danny nodded. 'Danny?' She was definitely confused.

'I'll see you later,' Danny said quietly as he turned and headed back out into the yard.

He found Scott feeding the chickens. 'Come on, let's pack it in.'

'Eh?'

'She's off her rocker,' Danny told him. 'She threatened me with her shot-gun. I've had it.'

'What do you mean, she threatened you?' Scott threw another handful of grain to the chickens.

'She can't even remember who I am,' Danny said in disgust. 'Anyway, I can't stand the thought of funerals and all that hassle. I'm moving on.'

'To where?'

'Anywhere. So long as it's out of here.' When he saw that Scott was looking at him doubtfully, he said, 'You don't believe me, do you?' He pointed back at the house. 'Well, *you* go in there, then, and get *your* brains blown out.'

'All right,' Scott said, putting down the grain container. 'I will.'

In the kitchen, Mrs Forbes was sitting at the table – and it was as if time had spun backwards, and they had just come in again from the gate where the old man in the van had told them that Mrs Forbes had lost her husband. There were

114

the things spread out on the table, the watch, the wallet, the spectacles and the penknife. There was the photograph, which she showed them. 'We used to laugh when we were alone,' she said with a smile. 'Ned used to say we were Darby and Joan against the world.' Then, suddenly, the smile faded. She pushed her chair back and stood up. 'Who the hell are you?' she demanded ferociously, watching them as she backed towards the corner where her shot-gun was standing. 'Throw stones on my roof, will you?' They could only stare at her in amazement as she grabbed the shot-gun and pointed it at them. 'Well, not any more, you don't,' she said in a strange, cracked voice.

The twin barrels were pointing straight at them. Her finger was on the trigger. 'That's an old gun, Mrs Forbes,' Scott said nervously.

'Yes . . .' She lowered the gun and studied it as if seeing it for the first time. 'Yes, it is old.'

'Can I see it?' Scott moved slowly towards her. 'Can I have a look?'

Danny was holding his breath. It was a tense moment. At any instant, she could bring up the gun again, her finger tightening on the trigger . . . She didn't know what she was doing. Then, to his surprise, she was handing the gun to Scott. 'Ah . . . you boys . . . you . . . you'd better get back to work,' she said haltingly and in a puzzled tone. Turning, she walked out of the kitchen to her

115

bedroom.

'See?' Danny said softly to Scott who was replacing the gun in the corner. 'She *is* off her rocker. Let's get out of here.'

Scott shook his head. 'We can't leave her like that,' he said grimly. 'You heard what she said. She's got no relatives, no friends. She's completely alone.'

'Well, that's not our fault,' Danny countered. It would be much simpler if they could just leave, put the old woman miles behind them. But maybe Scott was right. 'Okay, so what do we do then? I reckon we should call a doctor.'

'We can't do that. They'll put her away.'

'So they should,' Danny said shortly. He had had quite a fright just then; he was still getting over it. 'She can't go wandering about like that.'

'What if it's only a temporary thing,' Scott pointed out, 'and she snaps out of it? What then?'

Danny wished Scott wouldn't throw up all these objections; he wasn't making it easy at all. 'They'd let her go. This isn't the dark ages – and if she is a bit senile, she needs professional help.'

'Okay,' Scott said after a moment's consideration. 'But we're going to wait until after the funeral. And if you don't like it, you can get out.'

The funeral was very brief and simple. It was lonely – and touching. Scott, Danny and Mrs Forbes were the only mourners. Two grave diggers stood directly to one side as the minister

116

read the service. When it was over, Mrs Forbes threw the bunch of flowers she was holding onto the coffin. Scott and Danny were wearing the shirts and ties they had bought in the town from their wages.

When he came for breakfast the following morning, Danny found that Scott was already in the kitchen, talking to Mrs Forbes who was frying sausages and eggs in a large pan at the stove.

'Oh, there you are,' the old woman greeted him. 'Slept in, did you?'

'Yeah.' It was the country air that made him sleep like a log. He sat down at the table. He and Scott ate in the kitchen now instead of the barn. The smell of the food made him realise how hungry he was.

'And what about you, Danny?' Mrs Forbes asked.

'What about me?'

'Mrs Forbes was just asking what we're going to do with our lives,' Scott explained.

'I don't know,' Danny replied. 'I'm not going to be a plumber like the old man, that's for sure.'

'So he's a plumber now?' Mrs Forbes cast a shrewd glance at Scott. 'A minute ago he was an engineer.'

Danny suddenly had a sinking feeling. Scott would have mentioned the fact that *his* old man was an engineer. Then, before he could find an excuse, and he was trying very hard, Mrs Forbes

117

tapped the side of her head with her forefinger.

'I'm getting a bit forgetful. You're both brothers, aren't you?'

'Thats right,' Danny answered.

'And your father was always taking a stock whip to you.'

'Well... not exactly a stock whip.'

'He punched you then.'

They were on sticky ground again. 'Ah... well, it's all history now,' Danny said uneasily. 'We're just not going back there.'

The sausages sizzled in the pan. Mrs Forbes frowned in concentration. 'He told me to tell you something...' *Now* what was she talking about? 'It was all right.'

'What was, Mrs Forbes?'

She was still making an effort to concentrate. 'I can't remember...' She shook her head. 'No, I can't remember.'

She was off again. One minute she was as right as rain, then the next, she was way off beam. But she was harmless enough, even if she did point a shot-gun at them that day. Well, basically harmless, anyway, Danny thought.

Now that they decided to stay, there was plenty of work for them to do. When Mrs Forbes pointed out one of the fields and told them that was where she and her husband had once grown vegetables to sell to the motorists who passed by, and suggested they should be planning to do

118

something like that again, they thought it was a good idea. They could set up a stall at the side of the road, and sell the vegetables. But first they had to prepare the ground, and plant the seeds.

They enjoyed working on the farm. It was a good, healthy life. Ramsay Street was behind them, and when they did think of their homes, it was with some regret that things had turned out the way they had, and they guessed their parents must be still worried sick by their disappearance, but that couldn't be helped because they had made up their minds that they were not going back. Sooner or later their families would come to accept that.

Another job that had to be done was to clear out the shed which was full of rubbish. They were doing this one day when they saw Mrs Forbes emerge from the house with a stranger. It was a surprise to them because they had been so busy that they hadn't noticed anyone coming to the farm. They ducked back into the shed before the stranger could see them. It could mean trouble.

Mrs Forbes and the stranger paused near the shed. Mrs Forbes would have known that Scott and Danny were in the shed. The stranger was tall and bald, and was wearing a suit.

'We waited as long as we could before we bothered you, Mrs Forbes,' he said in a high, rather reedy voice. 'But now... well, now we have to decide what's going to happen to the farm. You must admit it *is* run-down, and you couldn't possibly manage it on your own.'

From inside the shed, Danny and Scott noticed him studying an old rusty milk churn they had dragged out only moments earlier. 'We used to sell our milk in the village,' Mrs Forbes said dreamily. 'It was a village then.'

'About selling the farm,' the stranger said impatiently. 'The bank has to recover its money, of course.'

'Yes, you're right,' she said meekly, and Danny was surprised she wasn't putting up a fight. 'I couldn't manage it on my own.' She stared around her, at the fields, the house, the barn. 'If you prepare the papers,' she said resignedly as they moved on, 'I'll sign them.'

Shortly after that Mrs Forbes received another visitor. This time it was a woman social worker who had come to arrange for the old lady to be looked after properly when she left the farm.

'It looks as if they've found me a nice place to stay,' she wistfully told the boys later. 'She was talking about a nice, comfortable hostel at Ballyvale where I'd be well looked after together with people of my own age.' She looked at each of them closely for a long moment. 'You two may as well go home now. There's nothing more for you to do here. Go on.' She made a quick brushing gesture with one gnarled hand. 'Swallow your pride, call your family. Ask them to come and get you.'

Scott turned to Danny. 'Maybe she's right,' he said uncertainly. 'Maybe I should call my Dad . . . *our* Dad . . .,' he amended hastily.

Danny noticed the old lady's eyes narrow a little at Scott's slip. 'Oh, great . . . fantastic,' he said drily. 'You know what he'll do to us.'

'No . . . We should go back.'

Danny shook his head. 'There's no way I'm going to cop it for something I didn't do,' he said with grim determination. But, all the same . . .

'You don't fool me,' Mrs Forbes said sharply. 'Not for one moment. You two are not brothers.' The boys said nothing. It had been too hard for them to keep up a pretence like that for any length of time; there were too many pitfalls. 'Good mates – yes,' the old woman went on. 'But I can tell you've got different blood in you.' Her bleary eyes passed over them. 'And I've seen you without your shirts, and I couldn't see any scars, the marks that should have been there if you'd had all those beatings from this father of yours you told me about.' She chuckled softly. 'I'm an old woman, but you can't fool me.' She looked at Scott. 'I saw your watch that day, when it fell off the fence. There was a name and telephone number on it. I rang the number and spoke to a man who said he was your father. He sounded very worried. He said you could go back home because everything was all right. But I . . . I'm a

121

selfish old woman, I suppose. I didn't want you to go, because there was still work to be done – and I didn't tell you. I didn't tell him where you were, either. I'm sorry.'

'We won't leave until we know you're being looked after properly,' Scott assured her warmly.

Mrs Forbes smiled at them. 'Very nice of you, I'm sure – but I'll be all right. You know, having you two around ... at this time ... was like being granted a new lease of life. But whether we like it or not, it's all over now.' She stood up and crossed to the sideboard. 'I want you to have these.' She handed the old pocket watch to Scott, then the penknife to Danny. 'Just something to remember me by. They were my husband's most cherished possessions.'

Danny was overwhelmed. 'Then *you* should keep them, Mrs Forbes.'

'No,' she said solemnly. 'He would have wanted you to have them.' Her eyes were moist, and there was a catch in her voice. 'Now get out of here, quick smart, or I'll take the shot-gun to you both. And I mean it.'

The boys hesitated. Danny felt quite choked up. Mrs Forbes waved them away. 'Go on, away you go. It's finished, it's over. You've got your lives to lead, so go on out now and do it. Just leave me be.'

The Robinsons had a dog once, but he had died, had had to be put down, in fact – and that had been sad for everyone, particularly Lucy who at her very young age, hadn't been able to understand why this should have had to happen. But Digby had eaten a poisoned bait, and had been in great agony. Even now Lucy couldn't understand why her pet had had to die. She still blamed her father.

After Digby, Jim Robinson had vowed there would be no more pets. People – children, in particular – became too attached to pets, and if anything happened to them, as had happened to Digby who had been thrown a poisoned bait over the fence ... No, it had happened with Digby; it wouldn't happen again.

One evening Lucy came home in a state of distress; she had just seen a dog hit by a car around the corner in Bedford Street. The car hadn't stopped, and the dog was still lying in the gutter where it had been thrown by the impact. She pleaded with her father to go and see if it was still alive.

It was alive. It lay there, panting and staring moistly up at Jim. There was some blood, but not much. It was an old dog, of uncertain breed, and Jim couldn't tell how badly it had been hurt. The thing to do, he said, was to take it straight down to the vet to see what could be done.

After he had examined the dog, the vet reported that its leg was broken, but its skull wasn't fractured, as he had first suspected. But it was concussed and he wondered, considering its age, if it was worthwhile taking the trouble to save it –and, of course, Lucy, who had come to the clinic with her father, insisted that it should be saved.

'He's sick, darling,' Jim told her gently. 'And he's had a good innings – anyone can see that.'

Lucy appealed to the vet. 'You could make him better, though.'

There were a few other people in the waiting room, with sick dogs and cats, and even a parrot in a cage. 'He's very old,' the vet pointed out to Lucy. 'It wouldn't be fair...'

But Lucy knew what was fair, and what wasn't. 'How would *you* like it,' she demanded heatedly, 'if you were old, and they wanted to kill *you* just because you had a broken leg, or something?'

Jim could see she was upset. 'But it's different

for dogs,' he said, squatting down so that his face was level with her's and placing his hands on her shoulders. 'Sometimes it's kinder to let them go.'

She was pouting. 'That's what you said about Digby, and *he* wasn't even very old.'

'The RSPCA would never find a home for him,' the vet told her.

'He'll have a home with us.'

'No, darling.' Jim straightened. 'I'm sorry.'

Then Lucy became petulant. Her face contorted in anger. 'You *hate* dogs,' she cried. 'You killed Digby, and now you want to kill this one.'

'That's enough, Lucy.'

'I hate you.' Lucy turned and ran out of the waiting room.

'All right,' Jim instructed the vet as he prepared to follow her. 'Save the stupid thing.'

So the dog was saved. Lucy could hardly sleep that night because, as she said in the morning when she came in for breakfast, she had been too worried about Robert.

'Who?'

'The dog I found. Robert. Well, he has to have a name.'

'Why Robert?'

'Well, I found him in Bedford Street, didn't I? Bedford rhymes with Redford – so I called him Robert.'

She couldn't eat her breakfast when Julie placed it in front of her. 'Look,' Jim suggested.

'Why don't I ring up and find out how he's getting on?'

Lucy's eyes reflected sudden hope. 'Could you?'

The dog was fine, he reported a few minutes later, after having called the clinic. Relieved by the news, Lucy began to eat her breakfast. 'When can we pick him up?'

'We're not,' Jim told her.

She stopped eating. 'Why not?'

'Because he's not ours. He must belong to someone.'

'They certainly don't care about him,' Lucy said peevishly.

Jim was sitting opposite her at the table. 'Lucy,' he said firmly, 'we're *not* having another dog.'

Then Julie was siding with her sister. 'Oh, come on, Dad. It wouldn't hurt. It would be good to have a little dog again.'

'That's what you say every time.' Jim shook his head. 'Sure, it's nice to have a pet, but too many hearts get broken when something goes wrong.'

'I suppose so,' Julie said thoughtfully and she, too, was probably thinking of Digby.

'Well, it took you weeks to get over Digby,' Jim reminded her as he buttered himself another slice of toast.

'He didn't have to die,' Lucy muttered bitterly.

Jim bit into the toast. 'No, Lucy, we're not

126

keeping that old dog. I'm going to ring the clinic and tell them to find him a decent home. Otherwise, it goes straight to the RSPCA.'

Lucy was upset again. She glared at her father with unbridled hatred. 'And if no one claims him,' she yelled, springing up from the table and running into the living room, 'they'll kill him. I *know* they'll kill him.'

Julie also got up. 'I'll go,' she said to her father as she followed Lucy.

'They don't understand,' Helen said when they had gone.

Jim was feeling quite miserable himself about Lucy's outburst. 'Oh, it's easy for them,' he said with a sigh. 'They don't have to bury the little blighters.'

Helen nodded. 'They think you had Digby put down because he dug up the garden.'

Jim could hear Julie talking quietly to Lucy in the other room. 'How could I possibly tell them that he went through such an enormous amount of pain because some maniac decided to bait him?' He stood up and walked into the living room. He had made up his mind. He had been defeated yet again. Julie and Lucy fell silent when he appeared in the doorway. 'All right,' he said. 'You win. Julie, do me a favour, will you. Go to the vet and pick up the dog.'

Lucy gave a squeal of delight and threw herself into Julie's arms – and Julie looked equally pleased.

Lucy went with her to the clinic. 'Isn't he beautiful?' Lucy exclaimed when they brought the dog home – and Jim didn't think he looked beautiful at all; he looked quite mangy, in fact. Julie thought so, too; he hadn't turned out to be quite the adorable little puppy she had been led to expect, she told Jim. More than that – he smelled. But to Lucy, he didn't smell. To Lucy, Robert was beautiful. She fussed over him, and made him a bed of old blankets in one corner of the kitchen, at which Julie protested, saying it was unhealthy for him to be in the kitchen, that he should be in either the laundry or the garage.

When she took the dog out into the back yard, Lucy called across to Max Ramsay, in his own yard, to come and have a look at him. Jim and Julie had followed Lucy out of the house. Coming across to the fence, Max leaned over it and looked at the dog. 'Where did you get him?' he asked.

Jim told him, then said, 'I'm going to see if I can find the owner.'

'Well, I think I can help you there,' Max said. 'I did a job for an old guy in Bedford Street once, and I'm pretty sure that's his dog. His name was Graham, if I remember rightly.'

Lucy was dismayed. 'But he *can't* be someone else's,' she wailed.

Max looked uncertainly at Jim. 'Oh, I'm sorry,

Jim,' he muttered. 'I didn't realise ...'

'It's all right, Max,' Jim reassured him. 'Lucy knows that we have to try and find the right owner.'

Lucy stared woefully at Max. 'Are you *sure* it's the same dog?'

'Pretty sure, Lucy.'

'There you are,' Julie said to her sister. 'It had to belong to someone.'

'But why would they let him run out into the road like that?' Lucy wanted to know.

'You know how difficult it is to keep a dog inside,' Jim told her.

'And I'm pretty sure Mr Graham doesn't know what's happened to Patch,' Max supplied.

'Patch?'

'I think that's his name,' Max said. 'Yep, the poor old man will be worried sick. That dog's his life, you know.'

Well, it was something to go on at least. 'We'd better get over there straight away,' Jim said. 'Do you know the address, Max?'

'Bedford Street. Number 25, I think.'

Jim turned to Lucy. 'Do you want to come?'

Lucy looked down at the dog she was holding in her arms. 'Is Patch coming, too?'

Jim shook his head. 'I don't think there's any point in disturbing him until we're sure.'

That seemed to give Lucy some hope. 'Are you sure it's the right dog, Daddy?'

Jim didn't want her to have any false hopes. 'I don't know, darling. It looks as though he might be, though.' He moved back towards the house. 'Come on, we'd better check.'

The house in Bedford Street was very old and dilapidated. The lawn needed cutting and the flower beds were full of weeds. 'No wonder he ran away,' Lucy observed wrily.

'You can wait in the car if you're going to talk like that,' Jim warned her.

'Can I come with you ... please?'

'All right, but you leave all the talking to me.'

At first they didn't think there was anyone in the house. Jim knocked a second time, and they were almost at the point of turning away, to Lucy's quite obvious relief, when they heard a sound behind the door, which then opened to reveal an old white-haired man in a wheelchair. Lucy's face fell.

'Mr Graham?'

The old man nodded. 'That's right.'

Jim introduced himself, then Lucy. 'A friend of ours told us you have a dog.'

'Patch.' The old man's eyes were watery. 'Yes,' he said sadly. 'I did ... yes ... but I don't know what's happened to him. He's been missing since the day before yesterday.'

'I think we've found him,' Jim said.

'You have?' The old man's eyes brightened. 'Is he all right?'

'Well, he had an accident, but there's no real damage done. A broken leg and some concussion. We took him to the clinic. He's going to be fine. And now that we know where he lives, we can bring him home.'

'Could you?' The old man was clearly overjoyed. 'I'd be most grateful. You've obviously done so much already.'

Jim dismissed this with a wave of his hand. 'Not me. It was Lucy here. If she hadn't found him . . .'

The old man smiled at the girl. 'Thank you, Lucy, for saving my dog.'

By the time they had picked Patch up from the house and driven him back to Bedford Street, Lucy's sadness was tempered by the knowledge that they were taking him back to a home where he was loved and would be properly looked after.

Jim laid Patch down in a sunny position on the front porch. The old man in the wheelchair reached down to pet him fondly.

'Oh, just look at us two,' he said with a throaty chuckle. 'Don't we make a fine pair?' he examined the dog who was listlessly wagging his tail. 'Oh, you *have* been in the wars, haven't you?' He looked up at Lucy and Jim. 'It's funny how attached you can become to animals. I've had this one since he was a pup. My wife gave him to me just before she died, and he's kept me company ever since.' His hand caressed the dog as he spoke. 'He must have decided to go for a little adventure the other day.'

'He looks pretty loyal to me,' Jim observed.

'Yes, he is.' Suddenly, the old man thought of something. 'Heavens, all this must have cost you a fortune.'

'Not at all.'

'But the vet's fee ...'

'The vet does want to keep a check on that leg,' Jim told him.

'Yes, of course. I can make arrangements to have him picked up by the animal ambulance.'

'No,' Jim said. 'Just give me a call.'

The old man smiled and shook his head. 'You've done enough.'

'I think Lucy would like to know how he's getting on,' Jim said. He glanced at Lucy. 'It's time to say goodbye, darling.'

Lucy knelt down beside the dog and gently stroked his head. Patch's tail was still wagging. 'Goodbye, Patch.'

'Oh, not goodbye, surely,' the old man protested, then turned his head back to Jim. 'There's one more thing Lucy could do for me, if she would.'

'What's that?'

'Well, it seems old Patch has more life left in him than I thought – and, of course, I don't want him running out into the street again. So perhaps, Lucy, if you had time you could walk him for me now and again.'

Lucy's solemn expression vanished. 'Could I, Dad?' she asked eagerly.

'Of course, darling.'

'Thank you, Lucy,' the old man said with a warm smile.

But it still wasn't the same, Jim knew, as having a dog of her own, and when Helen started dropping hints that it might be good for Lucy at this time to have a pet, he put his foot down. No, he said, and why did everybody make him out to be such an ogre, when he loved dogs just as much as the next person? But he wasn't going to watch his kids become attached to another animal, then have their hearts broken when something happened to it. There would be no more pets, he said flatly.

He had just stated this to Helen when he noticed Patch's collar on the kitchen sideboard. It had been forgotten in all the fuss to have Patch restored to his rightful owner. Jim decided to take it back himself.

The old man was on his front porch with Patch resting on his lap when Jim returned to the house in Bedford Street. He was grateful when Jim handed him the collar, and said that he needn't have made a special trip. Then, conversationally, he asked about Lucy. Did she have any pets of her own?

'No, she hasn't.'

'What? No room?'

'It's not that,' Jim replied. 'We had a dog once, but it was baited.'

The old man grimaced in disgust. 'How can people be so cruel?'

'It put us off having another one,' Jim said.

'I often wonder who'll go first,' the old man said reflectively, stroking the dog on his lap. 'Him or me? I was so upset when he went off the other day. We've had a lot of years together now.'

Jim smiled; he was quite touched by the sight of the old man and his dog. 'You seem like good pals,' he remarked.

'Yes, we are. We've seen some good times, haven't we, Patch? You know,' he went on after a brief pause, 'I don't think I've ever been without a dog. As a kid, I brought home just about every stray there was.'

Jim smiled. 'We were much the same,' he said. 'I remember we had a sheepdog once. "Don't bring that dog inside," my father said. Then later on, "Don't think it's coming upstairs", then still later, "Don't think it's going to sleep on the bed". But, of course, it had these great soulful eyes – and you couldn't say no to it.'

The old man laughed. 'It's a familiar story. But you've got to admit that no childhood is complete without a pet of some sort. And dogs made my own childhood very special.'

He was right. Jim knew he was right. He

thought about what the old man had told him –
and he also knew that he wasn't being fair to the
others, Lucy in particular. Through his firmness
– his apprehension even – he was depriving her of
an essential component of growing up. He made
up his mind to do something about it. That
afternoon, just after lunch, he told everyone to get
themselves organised, there was somewhere he
wanted them all to go. He didn't say where; it was
to be a surprise.

Of course, they must have guessed by the time
they pulled up outside the RSPCA dogs' home
and they could hear the dogs barking. Yes, he said
with some self-satisfaction, he thought it was
about time for them to get a new family dog after
all. That was his surprise. Lucy was overjoyed.
She could hardly contain herself when he told her
to choose one for them.

And there were plenty to choose from. There
were brown dogs and yellow dogs, spotted dogs
and large dogs. There were dogs that looked like
toys, there were shaggy dogs and dogs with
stumpy tails. They barked and yapped, and
wagged their tails – and Jim knew that it wouldn't
be easy for Lucy to decide which one of them to
choose; he knew they would probably be there for
the rest of the afternoon – but he didn't mind in
the slightest.

8

It had all been so unnecessary – a silly mistake – and if that woman's purse hadn't been found in the bar where she had been drinking that afternoon, and returned to her, everyone might have been spared so much worry and strain – and Max might not have left home.

Deep down, Maria must have known that the truth would have had to come out at some time, but on the surface she had seen no reason why it should have to. It was a secret she had kept close to her all those years – but, there were times, more frequently in the past year or two, when she thought Max might have suspected something. Which might have explained his attitude towards Danny, always a source of concern for Maria. He might have suspected something, there might have been some sort of instinct at work, but he didn't *know* or hadn't known until the other day, when she had told Max the truth, and there was no secret for her to keep any more.

Not that it had been entirely a secret, she had to remind herself. At the time it had happened, and she had needed someone to turn to, she had told Helen Daniels next door – and Helen had understood, as Maria had known she would. But apart from Helen, she had kept the secret for sixteen years. Now Max knew – and he had left home because of it. He had asked her point-blank if Danny was really his son, and she had said, no, he wasn't.

They had been having a row about Danny. It was just after his disappearance with Scott, and Maria was unable to understand why Max shouldn't have been more concerned about it than he was. She had heatedly demanded if he would ever wonder why Danny had run away from home in the first place. Because he was spineless, Max had retorted, and Maria had exclaimed that Danny was her son, and all she wanted was to get him home safe and well, but by the way Max was carrying on anyone would think he was glad to get rid of the boy. He had denied it, but she had seen the guilt on his face and known she had struck home.

'All I know is that you've never shown him that you love him,' she had cried, 'let alone tell him. You've hurt him, Max, and if he's not coming back, it's *your* fault.'

Perhaps, if she had left it at that, if she had continued to live with the fact that her husband just seemed incapable of getting along with her son, it wouldn't have come out. But she was too distraught over Danny's disappearance – and it was a time when she needed all the support she could get, particularly from her husband.

'What have you got against Danny?'

'Nothing.'

'Don't give me that. I've seen you . . . all these years.'

'Can't we just leave it?' Max had been uncomfortable at her insistence.

'No. I want an answer.'

Perhaps he had really tried then to articulate his feelings, but hadn't found the way to do it. He had seemed to make a sincere enough effort. 'I don't know. I mean . . .' He had spread his hands in a gesture of apology . . . 'I *want* to . . . honest . . . but, somehow . . . I just don't seem to be able to get close to him.'

Something holding him back. 'Not even when he was a baby?'

'I don't know.' He had shaken his head thoughtfully. 'Not really.'

It hadn't been too late to call a halt, but it seemed as if she had been caught up in an impetus she had no longer any power to control. Perhaps it was self-destructive, perhaps not. Perhaps . . . 'Have you ever wondered why?'

'Of course I have,' he had said irritably. 'I mean . . . look, I'm not a monster, you know.' He had still tried to explain his feelings, which she had known was something quite alien to him. 'I mean ... he's difficult, that's all. I mean ... even you would have to admit that.'

'Is that the only reason?'

'Well ... yes.' He had looked up at her squarely then ... and it still hadn't been too late – not quite. 'No. Look, I mean ... right from the start I ... I was never really sure he was mine.'

So that was it, she was right. She had left him once; she had packed her things and left him. It had been springtime, and the trees had been full of blossom. 'I mean ... God, Maria ... he was only born nine months after you came back to me.'

Yes ... that was right. Maria had said nothing. She had seen the doubt on his face, the questions forming, something he *had* to know, once and for all.

And the one question she had known would come one day – and when it did come, it would be put to her directly so that there was no way of evading it, and she would have to tell him, and it would no longer be her secret ...

'Is Danny really my son?'

And ... 'No,' she had told him. Danny wasn't his son.

It had been a long time ago, but she remembered it clearly as if it had been only yesterday. She remembered green hills, a stream,

139

a stand of trees, and a stranger who had made her laugh.

Max had been hurt, angry and bitter. He had lashed out wildly at her – and she guessed she had always known that this would be his reaction when he found out. He had called her a whore, then stormed out of the house, slamming the door after him.

'I shouldn't have told him,' Maria said to Helen Daniels.

'Why did you?'

'Because he asked me. He finally asked me ... and then I just couldn't lie any more.'

'I know it's no consolation,' Helen said gently, 'but it might be better in the long run that he does know.'

Perhaps she was right; Helen was right about so many things. 'I think he could live with the suspicion,' Maria observed sadly, 'but he can't live with the truth.'

She had tried to explain things to him, but he hadn't given her a chance. There was no point, he had exclaimed bitterly. She had lied to him for sixteen years – how could he believe anything she told him now?

Shane knew there was something wrong between his parents, and although they tried to pretend that everything was normal, Maria knew he wasn't convinced. When he commented on how tired she was looking, she tried to dismiss it by telling him she hadn't slept well, that was all. But he was still suspicious.

'Oh, I don't know if Max is going to tell him,' she said miserably to Helen Daniels next door. She was crying. Helen had made her a cup of tea. They were alone in the house. 'It's an awful mess.'

Helen tried to comfort her. 'Blaming yourself isn't going to help very much.'

'I know, but this is the worst thing I could ever have done to him.'

'That's why he needs so much more time,' Helen suggested. 'It can't be easy for him to sort out how he feels.'

Maria dabbed at her eyes with a tissue. 'He ... he's a good man. I know he yells and screams, and ... loses his temper, but he's basically good ... and I can't bear the thought that I've hurt him.'

'Now he needs reassurance,' Helen said. 'He needs to know that you still love him.'

But for Max, it was too late for that reassurance. When she had tried to give it to him, he had rejected it because, as he said, he had been thinking, too – thinking of what it would be like in a week, six months, or six years for that matter, and the only answer that came up was that he would never be able to come to terms with it. 'And that being the case,' he said unhappily, 'there's no point in us living together any more.

The marriage is over.' He would leave the house, he said; Maria would stay on with the boys.

That was that, then. Maria was very unhappy about it, but that was what Max wanted – and perhaps he was right. But there was still the problem of the boys. How was Maria to explain it to them?

'I suppose all they need to know for now is that we're separating,' Max said, and Maria agreed that that was probably best.

'I want to tell Shane as soon as possible,' she said. 'Putting it off will only make it more difficult.'

Max thought about this. 'Perhaps we could do it tonight. I'll be out for most of the day.'

'I don't think he'll take it very well.' Maria had done all her crying; she was very calm now. Both of them were calm, quite matter-of-fact about the situation.

'He's old enough to cope with it,' Max pointed out. 'I mean, he'll just have to accept that we can't stay together for *his* sake.'

'And what about Danny? By the time he comes back, you'll probably be gone.'

'I wouldn't worry too much about him,' Max replied acidly. 'I mean, he'll probably think it's the best news he's ever had.'

But when they told Shane, hesitantly, neither of them found it easy. Maria at least had one worry off her mind because some crackpot old woman had rung Jim Robinson that afternoon to tell him that Danny and Scott were safe and working on her farm, wherever that was because she had refused to tell Jim where it was. When Shane learnt that his parents had decided to separate, he said he didn't believe it, it was the silliest thing he had ever heard. It took them some time to convince him that they were serious, and not making the whole thing up.

'But ... *why*? Why *now*?'

They couldn't tell him the truth – not yet. All Max could say was that he and Shane's mother had just somehow grown apart – and no, he hadn't met someone else, neither of them had met anyone else.

Shane was stunned by the news. 'But why so ... *suddenly*? Everything seemed to be all right between you two.'

'We've been thinking about it for a long time,' Max told him sombrely. 'It's not sudden. We just didn't want to say anything until we were certain.'

Then Shane became bitter. 'So after twenty years it's all over is it? So long, nice knowing you! Well, that's really great, that's fantastic.'

They didn't try to stop him when he angrily left the house; they knew he needed time to think. 'He'll get used to the idea,' Max remarked. 'It's bound to be a shock at first.'

Now that the separation had been decided,

there were practical details to be worked out. To set himself up in a flat, Max realised that money would be a little tight for a while, but there was no reason for Maria to worry about running short, he would make sure she wouldn't. When Maria suggested that she could get a job, that there was no reason why *he* should have to cope with it all, Max reminded her that it had been *his* idea to move out, so there was no reason for her to change her way of life on that account.

When Maria asked if he had decided where he would go, he said somewhere close, at least while the boys were still home, and with all his gear in the house, he didn't want to have to travel too far to fetch it when it was needed.

Shane helped his father move into the flat he had found, which, as Max had intended, wasn't very far away. He still hadn't gotten over the shock of his parents' announcement. He was querulous and insistent, and Maria tried to reassure him. 'Are you just letting him *go*?' he demanded.

'Nobody asked him to go.' Maria was exhausted; she had hardly slept at all during the past few nights.

'You certainly didn't ask him to stay.'

'No ... I didn't.'

'You're both like a couple of kids with a lousy secret,' Shane said is disgust. 'So what's the big mystery? Has someone been murdered, or something?'

'Don't be silly.' Maria's patience was stretched to its limits. 'Don't you think I would tell you if I could.'

'Then what's stopping you?'

'It would only make things worse. For you, and everyone else.' She turned and walked out of the room before he could press her any further on a subject which was almost too hateful to bear.

She kept thinking of Max and how he was coping alone in his flat. Helen Daniels tried to lift her depression by taking her to the movies, and although she didn't really feel up to it, she went along because Helen had been so insistent that the outing would do her good. She was worried, too, about Danny. Since that old woman had rung Jim Robinson, they had heard nothing of the two boys.

Then, suddenly, Danny and Scott were back home again – and Maria was overjoyed to see her son again. She had greeted him with cries of delight, kissed him a number of times to his increasing embarrassment, and generally fussed over him. Danny said he supposed he was due for some pretty heavy treatment from the old man when he returned home from work. Maria's smile faltered, then vanished.

'He won't be coming home.'

'Why? Is he working away somewhere?'

'No . . .' It would have had to come up sooner

or later, but she wished it didn't have to be so soon; the boy had only just come home from his escapade – and there had been an injustice there, too. 'Your father and I have decided to spend some time apart.'

'You mean you've split up?' Danny's eyes widened in surprise.

'For a time – yes.'

Danny considered this for a moment. 'Well, does he know I'm back?' he queried.

'I'll tell him.'

'It doesn't sound as though he'd care all that much.'

'You know he does,' Maria protested without much conviction.

'You reckon?' Danny regarded her quizzically. 'Where is he?'

'Not far. He's got a little place of his own.'

Danny laughed scornfully. Maria knew he was angry. 'So the great Max Ramsay has moved out of his own street.'

'Please, Danny...'

'Why did he go? It wasn't because of me, was it?'

'No,' Maria said carefully. 'We had a few problems, that's all, and we couldn't work them out together.'

'You mean he wouldn't talk to you about them.'

'It's not as easy as that.'

'Well...' Danny turned away... 'we can manage quite well without him, can't we?'

Maria didn't like the way he said it. She was sure he didn't mean it. She *hoped* he didn't mean it.

She was managing to cope, but she did miss Max terribly. There had been times, while she was still living with him, when she had been so exasperated with him, even to the extent of idly wondering what the place would be like without him. Now she knew – and she didn't like it one little bit. She knew that Max wasn't far away in case there were any real emergencies, and he did ring every day to check if there had been any messages for him. In the meantime, with the boys' help, she had to manage as best she could – and somewhat to her surprise, she didn't find it too difficult.

Then, one day, quite unexpectedly, when he rang, he asked if she would have dinner with him. There was something on his mind, he said, that he wanted to discuss with her.

He took her to a small Italian restaurant near the lake. It was dimly lit and intimate. Maria ordered lasagne while Max had spaghetti. They had a bottle of red wine. Maria noticed how tired Max was looking.

As they ate, he told her about his flat, and the neighbours on one side with their rock music going full blast at all hours of the night despite

Max's banging on the wall and his shouts of protest; and about the old woman who kept accusing him of taking her clothes from the line as well as anything else he could lay his hands on. Maria laughed, and said it sounded as if there was never a dull moment. Max studied her seriously across the red and white checkered tablecloth.

'I'm glad you could make it tonight.'

Maria dabbed at the corner of her mouth with her napkin. 'I've looked forward to it.'

Max nodded. 'Apart from wanting to say hello, and see if you were all right, I wanted to talk to you about the boys.'

'What about them?'

'Well, you know Shane's been round a few times,' he said. 'And every time he comes he gets onto the subject of why we've split up – and I think we owe both of them some sort of an explanation.'

Maria agreed. An explanation would have to be made at some time; there was no way the boys could be kept out of it. 'But we can't tell them the truth about Danny, either,' she pointed out. 'It would destroy him.'

'I don't know.' Max's smile was bleak. 'Sometimes I think he wouldn't mind a bit if he knew I wasn't his real father.'

Maria was hurt. 'That's a terrible thing to say. You're the only father Danny knows – and always will be.'

Max tilted the bottle of wine and studied the label. A waiter glided noiselessly past the table. 'I can understand him being riled about it,' Max said thoughtfully. He straightened the bottle and looked across at her. 'I mean, it seems I'm always taking my doubts out on him.'

'It's not too late to change it.'

'You reckon? Anyway, that's not the point. The point is – what are we going to tell them?'

The simplest answer to that, Maria had decided, was to tell them that she and Max just weren't in love any more. 'Do you think that will work?' Max asked when she suggested this to him.

'It will have to,' she replied.

And that was what they told Danny and Shane that same evening after Max had brought her home from the restaurant and Shane, no doubt hoping that the purpose of the dinner had been the first move towards an eventual reconciliation, had eagerly made them a cup of coffee. The simple fact of the matter was, Maria told them, that she and Max were no longer in love.

She couldn't really blame Jim Robinson for what had happened; he had assumed that Shane knew the real reason why his parents had separated. Helen had reported to Maria in great consternation that when they were talking about it the following day, Jim had asked Shane how Danny was taking it all, and Shane had told him that he seemed to be accepting it quite well. Jim, to whom Maria herself had confided the real reason for Max's departure at a time when she was very upset and Jim had offered his sturdy support, had said that he thought that given time Danny would come to terms with the fact that Max was not his real father. Maria had noticed that Shane was very withdrawn after that – and Jim, realising to his horror that neither boy had been told the truth after all, had told Max what he had inadvertently done. Then he came to apologise to Maria who, although apprehensive of the outcome, reassured him that it was perhaps for the best that Shane did know the truth about Danny.

Shane had been four years old when Maria had left home that time. He might have remembered her leaving, and being looked after by Helen Daniels during the time she was away – but he couldn't possibly know why she had felt it necessary to leave. He couldn't know the pressures of the time, Max's temper which took her many years to become adjusted to, her feeling of neglect – and then that awful row they'd had over a dress, of all things, which Max hadn't liked and had ordered her to change. She had refused, told him he was being silly, and he had stormed off to the pub...

She knew Shane had talked to his father about Danny – and knowing that they were discussing her, she had felt even more ashamed. She didn't know what Max would have told him; she didn't know if Max would be vindictive, and put the wrong ideas in the boy's head. And that morning, after Danny had gone to school, and Shane said to her in the kitchen that he could understand why she and Max had a big blow-up in the first place, what with his temper and all, but what he couldn't understand – indeed, what he couldn't stomach – was why she'd had to go overboard about it. When she asked him what on earth he meant, he said, well, it *was* a bit drastic, having an affair with another guy just because the old man had spent the night at the pub, which, his father had told him in the long talk they'd just had, was all he had done.

Maria was outraged. So Max *hadn't* told Shane everything; he hadn't told Shane about the woman with whom he had spent the night in one of the upstairs rooms at the pub. That was just like Max. She had told Max the truth when he had demanded it of her. Now Max had told only a half truth to Shane. And now she was stung into filling in the gaps.

Yes, to tell him about the row she'd had with Max that night, over the dress he hadn't wanted her to wear, and he had stormed off down to the pub – he had drunk a lot in those days, but he had always come back at night, and when he hadn't come back that particular night, she had gone down there to see if she could find out what had happened to him, and the publican had been embarrassed, and said, yes, well, Max had had quite a few that night, more than just a few, and he was sleeping it off upstairs. She told Shane how she had insisted on going to the room where he was sleeping, but the publican had become even more ill at ease and said she couldn't – and finally, when she had still insisted and was on the point of going upstairs alone to look for Max, the publican had blurted out the truth. She couldn't go up there, he had said, because Max wasn't... ah... exactly alone. And he hadn't needed to spell it out any more clearly for her than that. She had known that Max was with a woman.

'So I went home, packed a few things, and took you over to Helen Daniels. She was the best friend I had – she still is. She agreed to take care of you so I could be by myself for a while. I needed time to think.'

'Are you *sure* there was another woman?' Shane asked.

'Yes. He admitted it later. But it wasn't only the other woman. He was always jealous of me – and he never had any reason to be. He was the only man I'd ever known.'

Until... A small hotel in the country. Peace and quiet, and long walks in the fields, and through the trees, and by the banks of a stream. And there had been a stranger who had made her laugh, who had walked with her, and told her she was beautiful. He had made her feel like a woman again – warm and vital, desired and desiring– and then, two days later he had gone again. She had never seen him again.

Shane was looking at her incredulously. 'Are you saying it took sixteen years to bring this out into the open?'

'Max didn't mention it, I didn't mention it, and as time went on it was much easier not to talk about it.'

'That's all right for you and the old man,' Shane said shortly. 'But what about Danny? All this time, he's been the whipping boy.'

'You can't make me feel worse than I already do,' she said sadly.

He softened immediately. 'Look, I'm sorry, Mum. I'm glad you told me – I really am. It's just that...' he gestured uncertainly... 'I remember wondering why, all those years... what was wrong between you... and why he treated Danny the way he did.'

'I don't want Danny to know what I have just told you.'

'I won't say anything,' Shane promised. 'But one day he'll have to be told.' He looked at her intently, challengingly. 'It wouldn't be right for him to go through the rest of his life not knowing the truth,' he said.

Yes, Maria thought, Danny would have to be told. One day...

9

Des Clarke had just got rid of his mother and was looking forward to some peace and quiet, although he had to admit that he wasn't getting too much of that because even if his mother was no longer physically present in the house, her disembodied voice on the telephone maintained a connection that was equally unwelcome. But there was nothing he could do about it when she rang almost daily and unleashed a torrent of complaints about one thing or another. And then Daphne's grandfather showed up out of the blue, bringing with him a whiff of foreign and exotic climes and a parrot in a cage.

Daphne hadn't seen him for so long that she didn't recognise him when he arrived on the doorstep that day and apologised for not giving her any warning of his arrival, but he had just arrived back from South America, and God only knew what the wireless was like on those tramp steamers. He was a breezy, ebullient character who hadn't even had time to change his currency, and would Des mind paying off the cab ... Des didn't mind; he handed him a twenty dollar note.

His name was Harry Henderson. When he told Daphne he would check into an hotel later, she suggested, with a questioning look at Des who gave a reluctant shrug, that he might like to stay with them. Harry was pleased, and said he would take them both to dinner. Des noted that he had pocketed the change from the cab fare.

As he had promised, he did take them to dinner, but then discovered he had forgotten his American Express card. How silly it was of him to forget, he said – and Des paid for the dinner. Harry promised to reimburse him. Des didn't keep his hopes too high about that.

When Des suggested Harry could sleep in the spare room; in which he would set up a camp bed for him, Harry pointed out, regretfully, that he had this trouble with his back, you see, and a camp bed might be a little awkward. He really should sleep in a proper bed. 'Maybe it would be better if I booked into an hotel,' he suggested.

But Daphne wouldn't hear of it. 'You can have my room,' she volunteered.

'No, Daphne, you can't do that.'

Des saw he didn't have much choice. He offered his own bed. No, he didn't mind, he said faintly when Harry asked him if he did. It was fine with him – which it wasn't, of course, but

155

there was nothing else he could say.

In the morning, while Harry was still asleep in Des's comfortable bed, and after Des had spent a very uncomfortable night on the camp bed, Daphne asked him what he thought of her grandfather.

'Bit of a rager, isn't he?' Des muttered.

They were sitting at breakfast. Daphne was still in her dressing gown. 'What is that supposed to mean?' she challenged him.

'Well, he left me for dead last night, putting away the French champagne like it was lolly water.'

'You weren't doing too badly yourself.'

'Yeah, and I'm paying for it now,' Des groaned.

'French champagne isn't supposed to give you a headache.'

'I haven't got a headache. It's the thought of what it cost me that's the problem. I'm down to my last ten bucks.'

'You can always take out some more.'

'I only work in the bank, Daph, I don't own it.'

'Still it was nice of him to take us out.'

'But I paid for it.'

Daphne sipped her coffee. 'It's the thought, Des, that counts.'

'You know,' Des said thoughtfully, 'for a world traveller, he's a bit short of the old crisp and crackly, isn't he?'

Daphne shrugged. 'Don't ask me.'

'I mean, about the only thing he's got in his wallet is a picture of Elizabeth Taylor.'

'Well, he must have *something*,' Daphne said. 'I mean, he's always going around the world.'

'Do you reckon?'

'Don't you believe me?' Daphne frowned across the table at him.

'Well, I'm beginning to have my doubts,' Des answered. 'I think about the only boat the old boy has been on is a paddle steamer up the Murray River.'

'Don't worry about it,' Daphne said. 'Let's just give him a good time while he's here – okay?'

'So what are the plans for today?' Des asked.

'I thought we might go sightseeing,' Daphne told him. 'Then I thought I'd take him to the Senior Citizens' Centre where he can meet a few people of his own age.'

'Sounds like a good idea.'

There was a knock at the kitchen door. Then it opened and Julie Robinson's head appeared around it. 'Can I come in?'

'Hello, Julie. Of course you can.'

Julie looked a little uncomfortable. 'What's the problem?' Des asked her.

'Have you got a parrot here?'

'My grandfather's staying with us,' Daphne told her. 'He's got one.'

'Well, where was it last night?'

'I don't know.' Daphne looked at Des. 'Where did you put Squawker last night?'

'Out in the garden.'

'Right next to my bedroom window,' Julie said reproachfully.

'Is something wrong, Julie?' Daphne queried.

'No . . . only that it squawked all night and kept me awake. Didn't you hear it?'

'Not me,' Daphne replied. 'I can sleep through anything. How about you, Des?'

Des shook his head. 'Not after four bottles of champers.'

'Well, I can assure you it squawked and squawked under my window all night,' Julie declared somewhat testily.

'I'm sorry, Julie.'

Now Julie was sarcastic; there was little love lost between her and Daphne. 'It's all right for those of us who can loll around all day, but there are some of us who need our beauty sleep.'

'I'm sure you do,' Daphne said sweetly.

'We'll keep it quiet tonight,' Des promised.

Daphne and Harry didn't come home that night until well after ten. Des had fixed his own dinner, and when he went to feed the parrot it bit his finger. It was still painful.

'Where have you been all this time?' he demanded when Daphne, looking quite worn out, turned off the television and slumped into a chair.

'Everywhere,' she groaned, kicking off her shoes. 'I'm exhausted.'

'Where's Harry?'

'He's coming. He's out the back, talking to Squawker. I tell you, Des,' she went on dismally, 'inside that frail old body is a human dynamo. Art Gallery... museum... shops... lunch... Senior Citizens' Centre...' She ticked them off on her fingers.

'How did he get on at the Senior Citizens' Centre?'

'I don't know. I left him there. I think he had a good time, though. He told me he met someone there. A Miss Jones.'

Des chuckled. 'The old devil.'

'Maybe that's what he needs,' Daphne said. 'A nice old lady to take care of him in his twilight years.'

'What else did you do?' Des asked.

'We went to a five o'clock movie.'

'*On Golden Pond*?'

'*Last Tango in Paris*. It was a revival.'

'I bet more than the movie was revived!'

Daphne laughed. 'Then we had dinner. Then Chinatown where he signed up for a course in kung-fu.'

'Harry's going to learn kung-fu?' Des was startled.

'No. He's going to teach it. He says it's one of the ancient skills he picked up in the mysterious

East.'

Des heard the back door closing. 'No wonder you're tired.'

Harry had brought the bird into the house with him. 'Did you feed my bird?'

'Yeah,' Des replied ruefully. 'He bit my finger.'

Harry placed the cage on the floor. 'You must have done something to annoy him,' he observed. He smiled at Daphne. 'Anyway, I think I'll turn in now, love. Thanks for a marvellous day.'

'That's all right, Grandpa. Goodnight.'

When he had gone, Des yawned and stood up. 'Well, now that you're home, I think I'll go to bed, too.' It would be another uncomfortable, restless night on the camp bed. He looked down at the cage and the bird which was glaring balefully back at him. 'I suppose we'd better keep this animated feather duster inside.'

'Don't talk like that, Des,' Daphne admonished him. 'I think he's rather cute.'

'So was Attila the Hun,' Des muttered. 'I'm going to clean my teeth.'

The parrot squawked. Des couldn't sleep because of the squawking. Finally, in exasperation, he got up and went out to the cage. 'Shut up!' he commanded, and the bird squawked even louder. 'You do that again, and I'll glue your beak together.' There was another squawk. Des went to the bathroom and brought back a towel which he then draped over the cage. 'Now drop dead,' he said, and went back to his uncomfortable camp bed in the spare room.

In the morning, when he took the towel from the cage, he was horrified to see the parrot lying at the bottom of the cage with its feet up in the air. It was obviously very dead.

Harry was still asleep in Des's bed. Des knocked on Daphne's door. 'Something terrible has happened,' he said when she sleepily asked him what the matter was.

'Grandpa?' She came out of her room in her dressing gown.

'Worse than that.' He showed her the cage, and the bird lying motionless at the bottom of it. 'He's snuffed it.'

'Oh, that's awful.'

'I told him to drop dead. I didn't think the stupid thing would take me at my word.'

'What are we going to do?' Daphne whispered. 'It's going to kill Harry when he finds out.'

'Worse than that,' Des groaned. 'He's going to kill me.'

'He dotes on Squawker,' Daphne said. 'It's like one of his family.'

Something had to be done. It was still early; the shops wouldn't be open for another couple of hours or so. 'I'll do the rounds of the pet shops and see if I can't get another one.'

Daphne stared at him. 'You mean ... substitute another bird?'

Des opened the door of the cage and peered in at the bird. 'Sure. Why not? They all look the same.'

'I hope you're right,' Daphne said doubtfully.

Before he left, Daphne made him a cup of coffee. The towel had been replaced over the bird's cage. 'Look, when Harry gets up you'll have to stop him from taking the towel off the cage.'

'How am I supposed to do that?'

'I don't know. Use your imagination.'

The door opened and Harry, wearing a track suit, walked into the kitchen. 'Good morning, Harry,' Des greeted him, over brightly.

Harry regarded him suspiciously. 'What's up with you this morning?'

'Nothing. I just said good morning.'

'It was the *way* you said it. People who talk like that are usually up to no good.'

Des was standing between Harry and the cage. When Harry moved towards it, Des blocked his way. 'What's this?' Harry demanded gruffly. 'Some sort of dance?'

'I just don't think you should disturb Squawker,' Des said quickly.

Harry looked at him in a puzzled way. 'But I just want to say hello to him.'

'But he's dead asleep...' Des winced; it wasn't the right thing to say... 'I mean, he's asleep.

Don't wake him.'

'But he likes me to wake him.'

Des was close to panicking. 'Well, he can't. He's ... lying down.'

Harry glanced darkly at Daphne. 'Where did you find this blithering idiot?'

'It wasn't easy,' Daphne told him. 'Now, look, Grandpa, why don't you go out for your jog?'

'And Daphne will have breakfast ready for you when you get back,' Des said desperately.

Harry thought about it for a moment, then decided he would go for his jog. 'Now you'd better hurry and find another Squawker,' Daphne urged Des after he had gone.

It wasn't easy, but he did manage to find another bird identical to the dead Squawker. It cost him fifty dollars, but it was worth it, he decided. He brought it back to the house in a cardboard box which had holes punched in it. 'It's Squawker's twin,' he announced to Daphne. 'It's own mother wouldn't be able to tell them apart.'

He was about to take the lid from the box when the front door closed and they heard Harry singing 'I left my heart in San Francisco ...' Des positioned himself in front of the box so that Harry wouldn't see it on his way to his room. 'You ought to come running with me one day, son,' Harry remarked to Des as he passed the doorway.

'Yeah ... yeah, I will.'

The moment the bedroom door closed, Des whipped the towel off the cage. It was empty. The door was open. Des was astonished. He turned to Daphne. 'Did you get rid of it?'

'Not me.' Daphne was just as surprised as he was. 'I never touched it.'

Des stared helplessly at the cage and the open door and suddenly had a thought. He called out to Harry. 'Harry, how does Squawker sleep?'

'Same as I do,' Harry shouted back. 'Knees up, Mother Brown.'

'You mean ... on it's back?'

'That's right. Funny old thing. Sometimes you'd swear he was playing dead.'

Hells bells, he thought. 'I knew it,' he said to Daphne. 'I should have wrung its neck last night. Now the damn thing has flown away.'

Harry came into the room. 'Where's my towel?' He spotted the towel that covered the now empty cage. 'Ah, there it is.'

He was about to take it off the cage when Des took his arm and propelled him back into the hall. 'I'll get you a fresh one.'

Harry looked back at his towel. 'That one's fresh enough.' He shook himself free, and before Des could stop him, had crossed to the cage and lifted the towel from it. Des steeled himself for the expected outburst.

But there was no outburst. There was a bird

sitting on the perch inside the cage. Then, behind Harry's back, Daphne showed Des the empty cardboard box, and he breathed a huge sigh of relief.

Harry was squatting down beside the cage, talking to the bird – but the bird wasn't answering him. Harry was perplexed. 'Maybe it has laryngitis,' Des suggested helpfully.

'Parrots don't get laryngitis,' Harry snorted, straightening up and heading for the bathroom with his towel.

He had just gone when, suddenly, there as a loud squawk from just outside the kitchen window. Des and Daphne hurried across to the window, and peered out. Squawker was sitting on the fence. In the bathroom, Harry was singing, 'Oh, if I had the wings of an angel, over these prison walls . . .'

'Take the one out of the cage and put it back in the box,' Des ordered Daphne. 'I'll see if I can catch Squawker.' He rushed outside.

He managed to catch the bird, but not without getting his finger bitten again. 'He hates me,' he complained to Daphne when he returned to the kitchen, and placed the bird in the empty cage. He nodded towards the cardboard box in which the second bird had been placed. 'Now to get rid of this one.'

The bird squawked. Harry came out of the bathroom in his dressing gown, 'Oh, he's started

165

talking again. Hello, baby,' he said to the bird, then to Des, 'Can I borrow your aftershave?'

'Sure.'

Harry returned to the bathroom. Des took the cardboard box, opened the lid and released the bird. It flew away, fifty bucks of his hard earned cash winging its way to the back of beyond. It was a flaming tragedy.

When he was back inside the house, there was a knock at the front door. Daphne opened it. A very attractive young woman in a tight dress smiled at her in a friendly way. 'Is, Harry ... ?'

Then Harry, dressed now, was in the hall. 'Cleo!'

'Harry!' Harry gave her a hug. 'I brought our raffle ticket.' Cleo told him.

'Good.'

There was a taxi at the kerb. 'I have to pay the taxi,' Cleo said.

'Hold on, I'll do it,' Harry looked appealingly at Des, who with a resigned sigh, took out his wallet and handed him his last ten dollar note. Harry passed it on to Cleo.

'Who is she?' Daphne asked while Cleo was paying the driver.

'Miss Jones. The one I was telling you about.'

'The nice old lady who's going to look after Harry in his twilight years,' Des remarked drily to Daphne.

'But I thought you said she was from the

Senior Citizens' Centre,' Daphne said in some perplexity.

'She is,' Harry said. 'She's the telephonist.'

Then Cleo was back with the change from the ten dollars. She handed it to Harry who deftly pocketed it and then, with his arm around her, ushered her into the house.

They were carrying on like a couple of kids, giggling and being quite silly. Des and Daphne listened to them in Harry's bedroom, and wondered just what the hell was happening in there. Still, Des thought, as long as they were making a noise, it couldn't be too intense.

They were going out somewhere. 'I don't know what you think,' Harry said when they emerged from the bedroom. 'Us making all that noise.'

'You're only young once, Grandpa,' Daphne pointed out.

It was a jibe, but Harry ignored it. 'You're only as young as you feel – and at the moment I feel about nineteen.' He winked at Cleo. 'Frisky and bursting with vitality. So you had better watch out my girl.'

'I don't know about that.' With a jerk of her head towards Harry, Cleo beamed at Daphne. 'Do you know we're going around the world together?'

Daphne brightened. 'Good. When?'

'As soon as we win the raffle. Harry bought a ticket for us both – the lucky last in the book, and it's drawn today.'

They headed off together, arm in arm, the old man and the young woman in the tight dress who was about the same age as his granddaughter. Daphne told them to enjoy themselves, and they said they would.

When Des arrived home from the bank that evening, the first thing he heard was Daphne in the bedroom, telling someone to lie still while she tickled his tummy. Full of foreboding, he moved towards the slightly open door of her bedroom. Just as he reached it, the door opened all the way, and Daphne started when she saw him standing there. 'Oh, Des, you gave me a fright.'

'Who's in there?' he said darkly.

'What do you mean?'

'The guy you're tickling.' He was really expecting the worst.

'Oh, him. Hold on a tick.' She retreated into her room, and a moment later emerged again with Squawker in his cage. 'Tickling is about the only thing that will shut him up,' she explained. 'He's just about driven me up the wall all afternoon. I'm going to have to talk to grandad about him.'

Relieved that his fears had been unfounded after all, Des was suddenly depressed again at the mention of her grandfather. 'I ran into him today,' he said glumly. 'He tried to hold me up at the bank.'

'Held you up?' Daphne's eyes widened.

'What? *Robbed* the bank?'

It might have been easier if he had. 'Not the bank – me. He turned up with Cleo and pitched some hard luck story. It cost me thirty bucks to get rid of him.' He made a sound of exasperation. 'Look, Daph, I know he's your grandfather, but, God, I mean it's not just the money. He makes me feel old. I haven't seen anybody with so much energy.'

The parrot squawked. Daphne told it to shut up, and it squawked some more. Then they heard Harry's voice. 'I told you, didn't I? Squawker's just like a watch-dog.'

'How does he know you're back?' they heard Cleo ask him.

'Oh, he just knows.'

Then they were in the room. Cleo was bubbling over with excitement. 'Just wait till you hear what happened today,' she cried. 'Tell them, Harry.' She gave him a nudge.

'You know that ticket we bought for the world trip?' Harry was grinning at them expectantly.

'You won?' Daphne asked hopefully.

'No, not that, not the world trip. But we got to this restaurant for lunch, and there was this bloke there with a camera, he took our pictures, and all the customers jumped up, and then the manager came up to us . . .'

'With a bottle of French champagne,' Cleo interrupted.

'Yeah, it seemed we were the ten thousandth couple to go to that place.'

'We had the most fantastic free lunch,' Cleo said wistfully, and Des thought that a free lunch probably meant he might get his money back.

'But that's not the best part,' Harry said. 'The best part is that we won a free trip for two to the Gold Coast. We leave tonight.'

It didn't take Harry long to pack his things. Cleo helped him. There seemed to be a lot of giggling going on. Then they emerged from the bedroom with Harry's bags.

'Well, goodbye, my lovely granddaughter.' Harry kissed Daphne. 'I'll bring you back something nice.'

'Oh, you'll be back then?' Daphne asked unenthusiastically.

'Oh, you can bet your life. And you, Des – I'm trusting you to look after dear old Squawker.'

'And I'll look after dear old Harry,' Cleo said.

They moved to the door. Daphne and Des looked at each other. 'He said he would be back,' Daphne remarked when they were alone.

'I heard,' Des said unhappily, fixing the parrot with a hostile stare.